What was there about Jim Richards that seemed so familiar?

Andrea focused on his eyes, his nose, the shape of his face. His athletic build—broad shoulders, long legs and good looks. His bed-tousled hair. She recalled the warmth of his handshake and the moment of poignancy when he had placed his hand on top of hers. A tremor of desire shivered inside her. Why?

The man was an enigma, a puzzle with many layers and facets. Did she have the right to pry into his private life? Her sense of integrity said no, but her instincts kept tugging at her with a different answer. Every instinct she possessed told her he was not who he appeared to be, that he was hiding something.

Andi had to know who Jim Richards really was and why he had assumed a secret identity. The last thing she needed was to become involved with a mysterious stranger.

But she couldn't ignore his allure....

Books by Shawna Delacorte

HARLEQUIN INTRIGUE

COVER UNKNOWN

ABOUT THE AUTHOR

Shawna Delacorte worked for many years in television production until she turned to writing. With the publication of her first novel she was honored with the Waldenbooks award for Bestselling Series Romance by a New Author. Though she has lived most of her life in Los Angeles, she currently resides in Wichita, Kansas.

Shawna would enjoy hearing from her readers and may be contacted at 6505 E. Central #300, Wichita, Kansas 67206-1924.

Books by Shawna Delacorte

HARLEQUIN INTRIGUE
#413—LOVER UNKNOWN

Secret Lover
Shawna Delacorte

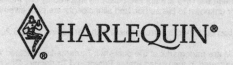

HARLEQUIN®

TORONTO • NEW YORK • LONDON
AMSTERDAM • PARIS • SYDNEY • HAMBURG
STOCKHOLM • ATHENS • TOKYO • MILAN • MADRID
PRAGUE • WARSAW • BUDAPEST • AUCKLAND

ISBN 0-373-22520-2

SECRET LOVER

Copyright © 1999 by SKDennison, Inc.

This edition published by arrangement with Harlequin Books S.A.

® and TM are trademarks of the publisher. Trademarks indicated with ® are registered in the United States Patent and Trademark Office, the Canadian Trade Marks Office and in other countries.

Visit us at www.romance.net

Printed in U.S.A.

CANADA

Vancouver
Island

WASHINGTON

OREGON

CALIFORNIA

1) VICTORIA, BRITISH COLUMBIA, CANADA
2) PORT ANGELES, WASHINGTON
3) PORTLAND, OREGON
4) ASTORIA, OREGON
5) EUREKA, CALIFORNIA
6) SANTA NELLA, CALIFORNIA
7) LOS ANGELES, CALIFORNIA
8) LA JOLLA, CALIFORNIA
9) SAN DIEGO, CALIFORNIA

CAST OF CHARACTERS

Jim (Richards) Hollander — Who is this mysterious man and why is he hiding?

Andrea Sinclair — Mystery writer whose fiction suddenly turns into reality.

Steve Westerfall — Is this investigative reporter after more than he's letting on?

Milo Buchanan — This powerful industrialist escaped prosecution once, but the case was never closed.

Gordon Conklin — Milo Buchanan's strong arm.

Keith Martin — Andrea Sinclair's agent—does he know more than he's saying?

Phil Herman — This prosecutor dismissed the charges against Milo Buchanan, then resigned.

Frank Norton — This ambitious assistant prosecutor stepped into Phil Herman's job.

Lou Quincy — He headed the U.S. Marshal's office, but is he bitter about lack of career advancements?

Ben Turner — The head of the FBI investigation of the Buchanan case had lots of expensive habits.

Sally Hanover — A computer whiz, with beauty and brains.

Theo Gunzleman — The court clerk had access to lots of important information.

Chapter One

"Mr. Buchanan, look at this." A sense of urgency rang in Gordon Conklin's words. He hurried into the large, mahogany-paneled office carrying a magazine. As with everything else that surrounded Milo Buchanan, the office reeked of money and power, from the thick carpeting to the leather chairs and the monogrammed silver cigar lighter. Gordon handed the magazine to the white-haired man of sixty-five seated behind the large desk. "Right there, Mr. Buchanan—the circled item."

Milo Buchanan was a slight man, his grooming impeccable and his manner fastidious. He picked up the magazine and read the circled item in the book review section.

According to his publisher, award-winning mystery writer Wayne Gentry's next effort will be a departure from his established style. Gentry, who has topped the bestseller list with his past five books, is basing a novel on the Buchanan Chemicals case of five years ago. He is centering the story around James Hollander, the missing government witness who was the key to the prosecution's case.

"Well, Gordon. Let's find this fellow, this Wayne Gentry. It's just possible that he's run across something in his research, some little scrap of information that we've overlooked."

Gordon's enthusiasm for the prospect of what lay ahead forced its way through his craggy exterior—fresh information, a new lead to follow. "Yes, sir, Mr. Buchanan."

Gordon Conklin had been administrative aide to Milo Buchanan for seven years. His primary function for the past five years had been exercising all avenues available in tracking down the elusive James Hollander. He used to be known as Gordie, and his mere presence struck fear in the hearts of many a hapless victim. Even though he now wore silk suits and reported directly to Buchanan, he had not given up his shoulder holster and .45-caliber handgun.

Gordon left the office, a look of determination on his hard face.

ANDI SINCLAIR STARED out the window. The snow had been falling for three days. It blanketed everything in a silent shroud of white, broken only by the dark, foreboding shapes of the tall fir trees that surrounded the cabin. She was not sure which was more disconcerting, the snow or the eerie silence.

She returned her attention to the typewriter and read aloud the words on the paper. "It was a dark and stormy night." She did not know whether to laugh or cry at the absurdity. *Of all the trite and ridiculous openings. I can't believe I actually typed that.* She stared at the words again. *At least it would have given my editor a laugh.* She ripped the piece of paper from the typewriter, crumpled it into a ball and dropped it on the floor with all the other discarded sheets. *Someone should be getting a laugh out of this, because I'm sure not.*

She hugged her shoulders and rubbed her hands over her upper arms in an effort to ward off the chill. She had been told that the winters were usually mild. This sure wasn't her idea of mild. What in the world had she been thinking of when she agreed to go to a small summer resort on Vancouver Island in the middle of winter? For the past six months her life had been in a state of complete upheaval. Ever since she broke up with Nick, her fiancé of two years' standing, he had been harassing her. Actually, *harassing* was not really the proper word. He had not been threatening her or anything like that, it was just…

Oh, Lord…I'm beginning to sound like one of the mystery novels I write—"Heroine stalked by obsessed former lover, film at eleven"—that's as bad as "It was a dark and stormy night."

Andi rose from the chair and stretched her five foot seven frame to its fullest, trying to get the kinks out of her back and neck. She had been sitting at the table for too long without moving. She kicked one of the wadded sheets of paper across the floor, shaking her head in dismay as she made her way to the fireplace. She had been putting off buying a laptop computer. She had considered it an unnecessary expense. Not any more. She planned to buy one as soon as she got home. She rubbed her hands together, then held them out toward the heat. The flames had died down. There was a supply of firewood stacked on the front porch. She reached for the doorknob.

A gasp escaped her throat when someone suddenly pounded on the door. She quickly yanked back her hand. There was no reason for anyone to be knocking on her door in this isolated place in the middle of a snowstorm. She started to reach for the doorknob again, then stopped as caution prevailed.

"Who's there?" She was not pleased with the quaver in her tone.

A smooth masculine voice answered her. "Andrea Sinclair? I'm Jim Richards, the manager and winter caretaker for the resort. It's been three days since you arrived and you haven't left the cabin. I thought I'd better check to see if you were okay. Is there any problem, or anything you need?"

Andi opened the door a crack and peered out at her visitor. He was tall, more than six foot, with hazel eyes and longish medium brown hair peeking out from the edges of his wool knit cap. His neatly trimmed beard and mustache were a slightly darker shade of brown. He appeared to be in his late thirties, although it was hard to tell with him bundled up in a heavy jacket, wool cap, snow boots and gloves. She opened the door wider.

Jim pulled off his gloves and extended his hand as he smiled. "We hardly ever get anyone up here in winter." He felt the tightening in his chest when their hands clasped as she accepted his handshake. The unexpected sensation immediately irritated him, but he covered the annoyance. He had become expert at hiding his true thoughts and feelings. He could not afford the luxury of allowing himself to be tempted by an attractive woman, no matter how much she caused his pulse to race. "What brings you here all by yourself?"

Her sparkling blue eyes held a look of caution. He could not call her beautiful in the classic sense of the word, but she had a captivating mixture of innocence combined with the type of sensuality that caused grown men to act like fools. The tightening in his chest indicated there was something special about her. Once again he shoved the unacceptable feeling away.

She quickly withdrew from his touch. The potent jolt of reality caused her insides to tremble. She stepped back from him in an attempt to regain control of this unexpected turn of events. "You startled me. I certainly didn't expect anyone to be knocking on my door, especially in the middle of this snowstorm. I was just about to bring in some firewood."

"Let me do that for you." He loaded his arms with several pieces of wood and carried them to the fireplace, adding a couple of logs to the fire. His gaze darted around the room, taking in everything, including the typewriter and the numerous crumpled sheets of paper strewn across the floor.

He returned his attention to her. "Are you a writer?"

His manner was open and easy. Her wariness of this stranger lessened, but the unnerving sensual pull of the man refused to go away. A nervousness jittered through her insides, caused not by any concern for her safety but rather the result of far more primal instincts. "Yes, I am. For the past four months I've been heavily involved in researching my next book and now I have to write it. I'm trying something different this time and I'm having trouble with it. I'm basing a fiction novel on a real-life case that happened five years ago. This is the first time I've tried doing that type of book, and I wasn't making much progress at home...."

Her voice momentarily faded as she thought of the reason for her concentration problem—the unwanted attentions of Nick. She quickly returned her attention to the problem at hand. Whoever Jim Richards was, he

seemed to notice everything—every detail that surrounded him. For some inexplicable reason she felt a
sudden need to let this stranger know that someone
knew where she was. "My agent thought a change of
scenery might be helpful in breaking the ol' writer's
block, so he sent me here—lots of peace and quiet
without any distractions."

He indicated the mess on the floor surrounding the
typewriter. "Do you have as many completed pages as
you do discarded ones?"

"Not exactly…" Andi allowed a soft chuckle. "In
fact, I don't have any completed pages." She stooped
down and began picking up the mess.

"Here, let me help you." Jim knelt down next to
her. She smelled good. It was not a sweet perfume
scent, rather a sort of crisp, clean fragrance—the type
that fit in with a snowy day in the forest. He reluctantly
acknowledged the little tremor of excitement that her
nearness caused. He looked over at her, his gaze capturing hers and holding it for a long moment. The tight-
ness in his chest returned. He forced his gaze elsewhere. "What kind of books do you write?" He
smoothed out one of the crumpled pieces of paper, then
quickly scanned the typed page.

"I write mysteries.…"

Jim heard her voice trail off in midsentence, but he
was far too occupied with what he had in his hand to
respond. The words leapt off the page at him—*Chicago…Buchanan Chemicals…dumping toxic waste…
James Hollander…car bomb, wife killed…disap-
peared…government still searching for missing key
witness.*

A hard lump formed in his throat and his pulse raced
almost out of control. It had been five years. He had

changed his last name from Hollander to Richards and, four years ago, had finally settled into these isolated surroundings. And now this woman appeared out of nowhere, claiming to be a writer and in possession of notes about his past. Was this Andrea Sinclair who she pretended to be, and was all of this some strange, cruel quirk of fate, or was the truth a lot more sinister?

He regained his composure and tried to focus his attention on what she had been saying. "Mysteries, you say... Have you had any published? I read a lot, including mysteries, and I'm not familiar with your name."

"I write under a pseudonym." Something about his manner touched a note of discomfort and suspicion deep inside her. Maybe it was from having had twelve mysteries published. She paused in her thoughts as she realized that the James Hollander book would be her thirteenth. She dismissed the silly superstition and returned to her original thought. Perhaps it was from her degree in journalism and the year she spent as assistant to Steve Westerfall, a top investigative reporter, that caused her suspicions. Her mind jumped at the many possibilities, ticking off a list of five different plots in the space of about thirty seconds.

"Really? What's your pen name?" He was only half listening to what she had said. "Maybe I've read some of your work." A disturbing thought grew inside him. What if she was one of those investigative reporters? He tried to dismiss the idea. If the United States government had not been able to find him hiding out in the Canadian woods, how could some reporter track him down? Then an even more frightening thought occurred to him. What if she worked for Milo Buchanan? No one would ever suspect a *woman* of being...

"I write under the name of Wayne Gentry." She was acutely aware that he was paying no attention to what she was saying. He just kept staring at the sheet of paper. She moved closer to him, anxious to see exactly what was written on that specific piece of paper that so captured his attention. She saw at once that it was some of her notes on James Hollander, the real-life counterpart to the main character in her book.

"Wayne Gentry? You're Wayne Gentry? That's quite a surprise. I've read some of your books. I had no idea they had been written by a woman. Why do you use a man's name rather than your own?"

Andi laughed, a relaxed laugh, indicating her discomfort had been somewhat alleviated even though her senses were still on full alert. "My first book was actually a police procedural. My agent said it would sell better if people thought it was written by a man. After that, even though my books evolved into straight mysteries rather than police procedurals, I was stuck with the name. The publisher hands out a bio that's as much fiction as my books."

"And this new book you're working on—" he tried to keep his voice calm and his speech patterns smooth and casual "—you say it's based on a real case?"

"Yes, the Buchanan Chemicals indictments." She cocked her head, narrowed her eyes slightly and furrowed her brow in thought as she stared at him for a moment. Something about him seemed familiar, something around the eyes. She tried to ignore the errant thought, but it would not quite go away.

She continued with her response to his question. "Of course, the case may not have gotten as much publicity here in Canada as it did in the States. Do you remember reading about it? It took place in Chicago about five years ago.''

''Yes…I think I do recall reading something about it. Wasn't the case finally dropped due to lack of evidence?''

''It wasn't lack of evidence, not in the strictest sense of the term. There was plenty of evidence, but the key witness disappeared. Without him, all the government could do was prosecute some lower-echelon hired help. The big gun, Milo Buchanan, couldn't be touched. And—'' she paused long enough for her next words to have dramatic effect ''—the case has never been closed. The government is still searching for that missing witness.''

There was an anxiousness to his voice, and his words came out a little too quickly. ''But, surely he must be dead by now. If the good guys haven't found him it can only be because the bad guys found him first, wouldn't you say?''

She remained silent for a moment, carefully turning his words over in her mind. ''I'm sure there are several people who hold to that theory, but I'm not one of them. I've researched this case very carefully, read everything printed about it and interviewed the police, prosecutors and government agents involved in putting it together. Everything hinged on the key witness, a man named James Hollander. He was Milo Buchanan's chief chemical engineer. When he found out what Buchanan was up to, he blew the whistle. It must have taken quite a bit of courage on his part.''

She paused for a moment, her brow furrowed and her lips pursed in a thoughtful manner. ''That's why I don't understand why he chose to disappear. He knew when he blew the whistle that he was in for a rough time, but he did it anyway. I just don't understand what happened after that. I couldn't find anything that explains why he suddenly broke away from his protectors and took off on his own."

"Maybe he didn't have any other choice." The words were spoken with a softness that made them almost inaudible. He shifted his weight uncomfortably. She had, indeed, done her homework. He felt the panic rising inside him. "What made you decide to do a book about that case?"

"First, the case is still open, which means I can put any type of ending to my novel that I want since I'm only using it as a base for my fictional story."

He stared intently at her. He did not like the direction any of this was taking. "And second?"

"What do you mean, *and second?*"

"Any time someone makes a point and prefaces it with the word *first,* that usually means there's at least one more point to follow."

She noted the very intense expression on his face and the way his intelligent hazel eyes seemed to be searching inside her. The power of his stare caused a tremor of apprehension to dance up her spine—apprehension of what, she did not know. The conversation had taken a very strange turn. Once again, the discomfort welled inside her. It was more than her undeniable attraction to this stranger. There was an inner tingling sensation nipping at her senses, telling her that things were not as they appeared. It was an instinct she had learned to trust.

She nervously bit at her lower lip as she ran her fingers through her short auburn hair, brushing the soft curls away from her face. "Well, that's very astute of you. You seem to have a very logical thinking process." Her gaze darted around the room, then lit on the kitchenette. "I was about to fix myself something to drink. Would you care for some hot spiced cider?"

Whatever was going through his mind was hidden behind his dazzling smile. "I'd like that. Hot spiced cider will taste real good on a day like this. Thanks."

"Make yourself comfortable and I'll have it ready in a minute." She silently acknowledged that he had been correct, there had been a second reason. *Obsessed* was probably too strong a word. She preferred to think of it as having become preoccupied with the missing witness, James Hollander. Was he not the honorable man he had originally seemed to be? Had he allowed himself to be bought off? Or was there something else, something her research had not uncovered? It was a real-life mystery in itself and one that she wanted to solve.

Jim took off his wool cap, removed his jacket and sat on the couch. He watched her as she busied herself in the kitchenette—opening the bottle of cider, selecting the spices from the cupboard, setting out two mugs. He was unable to pull his gaze away from her graceful movements—the way her jeans hugged her hips and the curve of her bottom when she bent over, the way her sweatshirt stretched across the fullness of her breasts when she reached up to take something from a shelf.

She was not at all what he had expected when he was told a lone woman had checked into a cabin for an indefinite period of time. She looked to be in her early thirties. Faded jeans encased her long legs, and a touch of color dotted her lips. A light sprinkling of freckles dusted her nose and cheeks. He forced his attention back to the blaze in the fireplace.

"Watch it—it's very hot." Andi handed the mug to Jim. Ribbons of steam curled around the cinnamon stick that protruded from the top of the cup.

He took it from her. "Thanks—smells good. Just the thing to take the chill out of the bones." He watched as she took a sip. Her long, slender fingers wrapped around the mug as she raised it to her lips. He closed his eyes, driving the image from his mind. Unexpected and potentially dangerous new matters required his attention, things far more vital than the way this woman drove his senses crazy without seeming to realize it.

As he watched Andi sipping the hot cider, he felt the first honest stirrings of emotional desire he had experienced in many years. He inwardly snorted his disgust at his wandering thoughts and yearnings. She represented life-threatening danger, yet he sat there fantasizing about her. Cabin fever, that was what it was. He had been alone for too long—alone and lonely.

"Tell me more about your book. Do you have some kind of an outline I could look at?"

"That's what I'm working on now...or at least trying to work on. I don't seem to be accomplishing much."

He chose his words carefully. "There must be several more interesting cases you could have selected for the basis of a mystery novel. You know, something like a big-time bank robbery or some sort of serial killer. A toxic-waste case seems kind of boring. Of course, you know your business—know what would be commercial."

"I chose it because the missing witness makes it a true mystery. I see it as a character study, a psychological story more than an action one. The ordinary man thrown into extraordinary circumstances. Not only is he blameless as far as any wrongdoing is concerned, he hasn't even been accused of anything. Yet in spite of that he still becomes the hunted man, on the run even though he's innocent. Where does he go? Who does he turn to for help? How does he spend his time? Did he manage to lose himself in the anonymity of a large city or did he seek a small rural community where he could just blend in, and after a couple of years no one would pay any unusual attention to him? He could be the short-order cook at a coffee shop, the clerk in a liquor store, the mechanic at a garage..." She gave him a thoughtful look. "Or maybe the winter caretaker of some cabins in the woods."

It took every bit of composure he could muster to keep from visibly reacting to what she had said. He told himself that she was just making conversation, not making accusations. At least that was what he wanted to believe. He forced an awkward chuckle. "Or he could pretend to be a mystery writer researching his next book."

She laughed. "Touché! You're right, of course. He could be anyone and no one would know the difference." Her expression turned serious again. "I'm really interested in the missing witness. Why would he have put himself in the precarious position he did by bringing Buchanan's activities to the attention of the authorities, then turn around and disappear the very day before he was supposed to testify? I want to know everything there is to know about him—his likes and dislikes, his hobbies, his family. From that maybe I can formulate a scenario that will extend a logical conclusion to an unfinished story."

She silently admitted that she also wanted to know more about Jim Richards, this intriguing stranger who had suddenly entered her life and caused her heart to beat just a little faster.

Jim shifted uncomfortably in his chair. He tried to project a casual exterior, but the tension coursing through his body would not allow him to sit still. He stood up, forcing himself to move slowly as he carried his mug of cider to the fireplace. He carefully formulated his words. "But wouldn't the government have already done a psychological profile on him? Figured out the most logical place he would have gone or what he would be doing—assuming that you're correct and he's still alive?"

Something tugged at her instincts, something was not right. It almost seemed as if he were trying to talk her out of the project. She tried to dismiss the thought as being ridiculous, but just like the other thoughts this one also refused to go away.

Her curiosity about him increased. "Well, enough about me. Tell me about yourself. This seems like a pretty isolated existence. I would imagine it's very busy in summer, but this time of year is different. Do you spend the winter here alone or—" she hesitated, not quite sure how to word her question "—is your family with you?"

"I have no family." The words were uttered softly in an almost expressionless monotone.

The silence hung heavily in the air. For a moment she almost imagined she felt the hidden despair his tone of voice revealed. She reached out and touched his arm, trying to offer a gesture of comfort and understanding even though she did not know what had caused his apparent sorrow. Her words were spoken just as softly as his, as if she were fearful of intruding into his private world. "I'm sorry."

He placed his hand on top of hers for a moment, then withdrew from the physical contact. "So am I."

He quickly recovered his composure and tried to shift the conversation away from himself and back to her and her book. He adopted a teasing manner, hoping to make the conversation sound light and casual. "I assume that Wayne Gentry lives in a stereotypical writer's loft in New York, but where does Andrea Sinclair live?"

She laughed at his question. She had never heard it asked in quite that manner before, giving her and her pseudonym separate identities and life-styles. "Wayne Gentry is a resident of the world. He lives wherever his desires take him. Andi Sinclair, however, is a little more conventional. She lives in a restored turn-of-the-century beach bungalow in San Diego—actually, just a little north of there, in La Jolla."

He liked the way she laughed, the way her nose crinkled. He gestured out the window at the snow. "And you traded southern California's sunny weather for this?"

She flashed him an ingratiating smile. "You're right, it does seem a little silly."

JIM STRETCHED HIS LONG legs out in front of him as he sat on his couch sipping a brandy while staring at the roaring blaze in the fireplace. He had returned to his cabin an hour ago, after spending a somewhat disturbing couple of hours with Andrea Sinclair—Andi, as she had insisted he call her. The more he tried to get her to talk about the book, specifically her research, the more she seemed to resist his efforts. He hoped he had not pressed her too much for information, causing her to become suspicious.

He felt fairly confident that she was who she claimed to be, not really comfortable but more at ease with the situation than he was when he first read the crumpled piece of paper. He furrowed his brow. If only he could figure a way to get his hands on the rest of her notes, determine how extensive—and accurate—her research was. There had been two books written about the case shortly after it happened, then the furor finally died down. The last thing he needed was a new book to stir everything up and once again focus attention on him and resurrect speculation about where he might be.

His mind drifted to thoughts he had long ago relegated to the darkest corners of his mind. There had been that very lucrative cash offer, tendered personally by Milo Buchanan with all the trappings of a top-secret clandestine meeting. All he had to do in exchange for the money was disappear before the trial. He had refused the offer and had reported the attempted bribe to Frank Norton, the Assistant U.S. Attorney working on the case.

Shortly before the trial was to begin, a car bomb killed his wife and put him into the hospital for two weeks. If he had been the one behind the wheel, the one who had turned the ignition key to start the engine rather than opening the door on the passenger side, then he would be the one who had been killed. The government put him in protective custody until he could testify and pressed him to enter the Witness Protection Program after the trial. He had reluctantly agreed, but the decision had been an uneasy one.

Then the day before he was to take the witness stand there was a second attempt on his life.

He had drifted into an uneasy sleep on the sofa while watching television. A sound—he didn't even know what—startled him awake just in time to see a large shadow of a man and the glint of a knife blade. Then a raspy voice, one he knew he'd never forget, told him Milo Buchanan sent his regards. The next few minutes were a blur in his memory. Somehow he managed to connect a solid kick to the intruder's stomach and escape through the back door. No one was supposed to know where he was...no one, that is, except for the government agents involved.

He did not know who he could trust. There was no one he could turn to for help. He was the only one who could testify to Buchanan's personal involvement in the dumping of toxic materials and about the bribe offer. Somehow he had to stay ahead of the people attempting to kill him while trying to figure out the identity of the person who had sold him out. For five years he had been running and hiding—doing what he needed to do to stay alive until the day he could see Milo Buchanan put away.

His thoughts turned to Andi Sinclair the woman. He abruptly rose to his feet and tried to shake the disturbing images from his head. He grabbed the fireplace poker and angrily jabbed at the burning logs. He could not deny his attraction to her, but a man in his position could not afford to become emotionally involved. It would be too dangerous for him. He thought back to the car bomb that had killed his wife. And too dangerous for Andi, too.

Chapter Two

Just as Jim had been consumed by thoughts of the time he had spent with Andi, she had also been unable to shake the disturbing thoughts that circulated through her mind.

She stared at the blank page in her typewriter. She had been staring at it for fifteen minutes without putting her fingers on the keyboard. Every instinct she possessed told her he was not who he appeared to be, that he was hiding something. She allowed a fleeting thought about her unexpected attraction to him but just as quickly shoved it aside. The last thing she needed was to become involved with a mysterious stranger she met one snowy day in the woods.

She had turned one particular thought over and over in her mind, though, and had finally made a decision. First thing in the morning, whether it was still snowing or not, she would venture out to find a phone. She was sure she could find one at the resort office. She allowed a slight frown. That might be a little tricky. It was probably where Jim spent his time, but she would just have to work it out somehow. She needed to make the call.

If anyone could get the information she wanted, it

would be Steve Westerfall. Not only was he a top investigative reporter, he also owed her a couple of favors and she intended to call them in. She would soon know exactly who this Jim Richards really was—if that was, indeed, his true name.

She visualized his face, tried to imagine what he looked like without the beard and mustache. What was there about him that seemed so familiar? Again, her mental image focused on his eyes, his nose, the shape of his face. Her mind drifted to the moment he had taken off his cumbersome jacket. She had been able to more clearly discern his athletic build—his broad shoulders, long legs and good looks. When he had removed his knit cap it had tousled his hair, giving him the very inviting appearance of someone who had just crawled out of a warm, rumpled bed.

She recalled the warmth of his handshake and the moment of poignancy when he had placed his hand on top of hers. A little tremor of desire shivered inside her, an unwelcome reaction to her thoughts. He was an enigma, a puzzle with many layers and facets. Did she have the right to pry into his private life? Her sense of integrity said no, but her instincts kept tugging at her with a different answer. She decided to go with her instincts. She would make that phone call first thing in the morning. She would soon know exactly who he really was.

"STEVE? ANDI SINCLAIR. I need a favor."

The man's voice on the other end of the phone teased her. "I'm fine, Andi. Thanks for asking. And how are you doing this fine day?"

She laughed. "Sorry. How are you doing, Steve? How are the wife and kids? Is the dog getting along okay? Did you ever get the cat fixed or is he still the terror of the neighborhood? Is that enough pleasant chitchat?''

"Stop already!" Steve Westerfall's good-natured laugh filled the phone line between New York City and the small resort on Vancouver Island. "Just once it would be nice if you started a conversation with something other than those dreaded words, 'I need a favor.'"

Her voice conveying a clearly teasing manner, she replied, "You aren't going to force me to remind you who entertained your sister and her family three years ago when they vacationed in California, are you? The trips to Disneyland, Sea World, Universal Studios, the San Diego Zoo—"

He returned her challenge, obviously enjoying the open banter that usually permeated their conversations. "Isn't this the fourth favor you've requested in exchange for the privilege of having my charming relatives in your home for that very short period of time?"

Andi affected a hurt tone of voice, as if she had been unfairly accused. "Of course not…it's only the third."

Steve's jovial tone fell soft and a hint of melancholy came through. "Yes, that was the last trip they were able to make before little Johnny…" He did not finish the sentence. There was a moment of silence before he recaptured his upbeat manner. "Enough already, I give up. What do you need?"

She quickly became all business, indicating the seriousness of her request. "This is probably going to be a tough one, Steve. I need a positive identification on someone, and I have very little information to give you beyond a name—Jim Richards—and I'm not even sure it's his real name."

She concluded her phone conversation as quickly as possible, telling Steve she would call him back in two days. Even though Jim was not in the office where she had found the pay phone, he could return at any minute. She did not want him to know she was suspicious of him. She did not want to alert him in case something was amiss, and if it did turn out to be just her overactive imagination...well, she did not want to embarrass him or herself, either.

JIM STARED OUT HIS KITCHEN window, keeping an eye on the door where he had seen Andi enter the office. Sometime during the night the weather had cleared. The morning was bright, the sky a brilliant blue with the sun glinting off the fresh cover of pristine snow. He had seen her slowly wade through the accumulation. He watched to see where she was going so early in the morning that was important enough to warrant fighting her way along the uncleared path. When she did not immediately leave upon finding the office empty, he assumed she must be using the phone—there was nothing else there to detain anyone.

He would have to take the chance. It would be risky, but too much was at stake. He quickly pulled on his heavy jacket, grabbed a snow shovel and started toward her cabin. Once inside, he kept a watchful eye out the window as he searched for her research notes. They were surprisingly easy to find, but then he reminded himself that there was no reason for her to have hidden them. There were three large envelopes, all marked Buchanan Chemicals/James Hollander. He opened the first one and quickly scanned the pages. He did not like what he saw.

Her research was very thorough. She had notes concerning interviews with numerous people from the Chicago police, the U.S. Attorneys office and various federal government agencies. The notes referred to interview tapes. The next envelope contained newspaper clippings, including a newspaper photograph of him. He studied it for a moment. It was five years old, the paper frayed and yellowed.

A certain level of anxiety jittered inside him. It was nothing too overpowering, but anxiety nonetheless. He reached up and scratched the beard he had grown to camouflage his appearance. He hated the beard but knew he did not dare shave it off. He had been able to convince himself that with the addition of the beard and mustache and his blond hair dyed brown that no one would be able to recognize him and certainly not from that old newspaper photograph—at least that was what he wanted to believe.

He glanced up just in time to see her emerge from the office. He quickly replaced the notes, unhappy that he had not had time to see what was in the third envelope. His gaze darted around the cabin, his mind working quickly. He could not return to his cabin without her seeing him and she would be back any minute. He quickly stepped out onto the porch and grabbed the snow shovel, busying himself by clearing away the three-day accumulation.

Andi looked up as she approached her cabin, the surprise on her face obvious. She offered a tentative greeting. "Good morning, Jim. Is there something I can do for you?"

He flashed a charming smile, as if his being there was the most natural thing in the world. "Good morning, Andi. Your porch needed clearing and your firewood supply replenished, then I'll be doing the path to the office and the parking lot. If you had waited a little while, you could have taken your walk without having to wade through this knee-deep snow.''

She impulsively turned toward the office and started to speak. ''Oh, I wasn't—'' She caught herself before finishing her sentence. ''How thoughtful of you. I must admit I was just wishing I had a pair of cross-country skis, or at the very least some snowshoes.''

The crisp, cold air seemed to heighten the electricity that crackled between them. It was a double-edged sword. On one side was a test of nerves with each participant unsure as to whether it was a solo contest or a competition. On the other side was the attraction each felt toward the other, a situation neither of them welcomed but one that could not be denied by either of them.

He cocked his head and arched his eyebrows, her words having captured his attention. ''Do you cross-country ski?''

''Yes, cross-country and downhill both.''

He leaned against the shovel and offered her an engaging smile. ''If you feel in need of a break from your work, perhaps you'd join me for a cross-country run this afternoon. There's a good hiking trail that starts on the other side of the parking lot, and it works just as well in winter for cross-country skiing.'' He was not sure exactly who was asking the question, the man who desperately needed to protect the anonymity that the appearance of this stranger had threatened or the man who felt a very strong attraction to this desirable woman in spite of the danger.

She reacted with surprise. ''But I don't have any skis.''

"That's no problem. There're several pairs here. I'm sure we can find something that will suit you."

"I'd like that." It would be perfect. If they were in a distracting environment, she could elicit some personal information from him without his being aware of what she was doing. She was a good interviewer, a talent she had developed while working with Steve Westerfall. She would get him to talk without his even realizing what was happening.

She glanced at her watch. "I'd like to get a few hours of work done, then I'll be ready for a break. Is that okay?"

"Perfect." He flashed her a dazzling smile that slowly faded as he reached his hand out and lightly touched her hair. He quickly regained his composure. "That will give me enough time to finish clearing your porch, the pathway and the parking lot."

TWO PAIRS OF SKIS RESTED against a tree along with two sets of ski poles. All thoughts of surreptitiously prying information from each other had been totally abandoned. The ski adventure had quickly turned into a carefree romp in the snow when Andi had impulsively grabbed a handful of snow and squished it in his face. He had retaliated by shoving her into a soft mound of snow, then pinning her down so that she could not get away.

His face hovered just above hers. His heartbeat increased and his breath came a little quicker. He moved his leg off from across hers. His voice conveyed a slight huskiness that surprised him when he heard it. "It's…it's getting late. We'd better start back—" he regarded her intently "—before it gets dark."

At that very moment, with his body pressing hers

into the soft snow and their faces almost touching, her insides began to tremble. She knew the feeling had not been caused by the cold, but rather by the unsettling anxiety that welled inside her again—a strange sensation that she had been trying to categorize from the moment of their first handshake.

Since her breakup with Nick she had thrown herself into her work full force. She had not dated anyone. No one had even captured her interest—until now. The snow may have been cold, but there was no mistaking the heat rapidly building inside her. Her gloved hand brushed the snow from his beard before coming to rest against his cheek. Her voice was soft and contained just a hint of uncertainty. "You're right...it will be dark soon."

He looked into her eyes for a moment longer, his mind filled with uncertainty as he pondered a decision. Then he lowered his head and captured her mouth with his. His kiss started out soft, almost tentative, but quickly escalated. Her lips were soft and supple. Rather than satisfying a hunger, her taste filled him with a need for more.

She felt the demand of his too-long pent-up passions, demands that stirred a sensual excitement inside her. She responded to his kiss, allowing it to continue for several seconds before breaking it off. There was no mistaking the heat that existed between them, nor was there any mistaking the hunger and desire conveyed by his kiss. She held his steady, unwavering gaze for a moment longer before saying anything. "Jim...we need to—"

"Yes, I know. It's getting late. We need to start back." He reluctantly rose to his feet and held out his hand to help her up.

While she brushed the snow from her clothes, he retrieved the skis. The conversation was slightly strained and a little awkward as they attempted to make small talk while heading back. Neither made mention of the kiss. It was as if they had both silently agreed that if they ignored what had just happened between them then they could pretend that the heated moment had never existed.

As soon as they got back, Jim returned to his cabin on the other side of the office from Andi's cabin. He had lived there four years, venturing as far away as Victoria, on the south end of Vancouver Island, only a couple of times a year. He had managed to make himself comfortable and had eventually become fairly content with things as they were. The summers were busy, the resort always full of vacationers. The winters, however, were long and lonely. He had welcomed the news of a winter guest, but now he was not so sure. She posed a definite threat to him, but he was not sure which was more dangerous: the very real physical danger or the possibility of an emotional involvement.

Andi, too, had retreated to her cabin. She tried to concentrate on her work, but her mind kept wandering to that moment when Jim's face was very close to hers, his body pressed against hers and his eyes searching into the depths of her soul, followed by the sensuality of his kiss. She forced the thoughts from her mind and turned to her research material. She had transcribed most of her interview tapes, bringing only her notes with her and leaving the tapes and complete transcriptions at home. She set about separating pertinent facts from useless information. She kept at it until her eyes grew tired and she turned in for the night.

"MR. BUCHANAN, YOU'RE NOT going to believe this. That Wayne Gentry guy is really a woman."

Milo Buchanan's head snapped up to attention at Gordon's words. "A woman? Are you sure?"

"Yeah. We got the agent's name. He's in New York. I had a couple of the boys go through his files and this is what they found." He dropped a file folder on the desk. "Her real name's Andrea Sinclair and she lives in California."

Milo Buchanan leaned back in his leather chair, a slight smile coming to his thin lips as he picked up the file folder. "Well, if she's a good writer then she must have research files." He looked up at Gordon. "Let's find out."

Gordon smiled, a crooked grin that suited his scarred face. "Right away, Mr. Buchanan." He hurried from the office, closing the door behind him.

Milo Buchanan reached for the humidor on the credenza behind his desk and withdrew one of the hand-rolled Havana cigars. He turned it over in his fingers, taking tactile pleasure from his illicit indulgence. He ran it across his upper lip, his nostrils flaring as he inhaled the rich and distinctive aroma. A contented smile turned the corners of his mouth. A good cigar and a snifter of excellent brandy were definitely in order. He closed his eyes for a moment. He had a positive feeling about this unexpected lead to James Hollander. At long last he would be able to close off that unfortunate chapter in his business dealings. He clipped the end from the cigar, then reached for his silver lighter.

AFTER FINISHING HER breakfast, Andi picked up where she had left off the night before. She was not sure how long she had been going over her notes when she was interrupted by a knock at her door.

"Hi." Jim flashed a friendly smile as he greeted her from the front porch. She stepped aside, motioning for him to come in out of the cold. The outward awkwardness and embarrassment of the previous afternoon's kiss seemed to have disappeared. "I'm going into the village a little later today for supplies and the mail. How is your food holding out? Is there anything you need?"

"Well—" she turned toward the kitchenette "—I don't think so. How often do you go into the village?"

"During the summer season someone goes daily. During the winter when there's no one here, I usually go once a week."

"I can't think of anything I need—" she gestured toward the table and extended a weary smile "—except maybe a computer to replace this clunky typewriter."

An amused chuckle escaped his throat. "I don't think I can do anything about that." His gaze traveled across the mess of papers covering the table. "How's it going?"

"I've been working on getting the story line together. I think I'm going to start the book with the second attempt on James Hollander's life shortly after he gets out of the hospital. From there I'll go back and—"

The look on his face stopped her in midsentence. She was not even sure how to describe the expression. It was a strange combination of total shock and absolute panic. "What's wrong? You look like you've just seen a ghost."

"Did...did you say *second* attempt on his life?" He forced his thoughts to focus, his mind reeling from the shock of what he had just heard. The second attempt on his life…no one knew about that, absolutely *no one.* He had not reported it to the U.S. Attorneys office, not told the Chicago police, not told the government agents assigned to his case, and not even mentioned it to the U.S. Marshals responsible for protecting him.

The second attempt…he had been assured that no one knew where he was being kept until the time for him to testify. At that moment it became crystal clear to him that he needed to get far away from everyone connected with the case, and put a lifetime of space between himself and everyone and everything he had ever known. He knew it was the only way he would live long enough to see Milo Buchanan put away for good. Everything in his life, all he had ever worked for, had been destroyed and he had been left with nothing. The only purpose left in his life was seeing that Buchanan got what was coming to him. It was the one obsession that had kept him going from day to day even when things looked their darkest.

And now, here was this woman who knew what no other living soul knew. No one, that is, except the man who had tried to kill him five years ago, the person who sold him out and Milo Buchanan, the man who had ordered the hit. He had not seen his assailant's face, but he knew he would never forget the voice.

He swallowed hard in an attempt to bring his rapidly building anxieties under control. He needed to be very careful in how he handled this. "The…uh…second attempt…I don't remember reading anything about it in the newspapers. What makes you say there was a second attempt on his life?" He did not like the way his voice sounded, did not like the apprehension he projected.

A wary look settled in her eyes as she spoke. "I was under the impression that you hadn't followed the case that closely. Did I misunderstand what you said?"

He attempted a casual manner, mustering all his reserve composure in order to maintain control. "You didn't misunderstand. It's just that I remembered thinking at the time how lucky he was to have escaped the car bomb. I can't imagine that he would have been lucky enough to escape a second—"

Too many memories, too much pain. He had finally achieved a feeling of relative security, the ability to function without jumping at every unexpected noise or being immediately suspicious of every stranger he saw. Only now, because of this woman, it had all come flooding back. Would it ever be finished? Would he ever be able to lead a normal life again?

"Jim? Is something wrong?" Andi reached out and touched his arm, unable to quietly stand by ignoring the painful expression that covered his face and the overwhelming sadness in his eyes.

"Jim?" Her voice was more urgent. She gripped his arm harder in an attempt to get his attention.

He quickly tried to recover from his lapse, to offer what he hoped was a plausible explanation. He extended an apologetic smile. "I'm sorry. I guess my mind just wandered. I was thinking about the things I needed to do in the village."

"Are you all right?"

"I'm fine." He attempted to press on for more information. "You were going to tell me why you thought there had been a second attempt on this guy's life."

She adopted a teasing attitude, hoping to put him off without making him suspicious of her motives. "No you don't. If I tell you everything now then you won't have any reason to buy the book when it comes out." She gently turned him around and edged him toward the front door. "You have to make a trip into the village and I have a ton of work to do. We both need to get busy." He turned back toward her, his eyes searching her face for something...but what?

He reached out and brushed a loose tendril of hair away from her cheek. "Will I see you later?" He recovered his composure, straightening his stance until he reached his full height. "Maybe another cross-country ski run?" He attempted a teasing grin but knew that he had not been too successful.

Her smile was open and easy. "Check with me later."

Jim left her cabin and went directly to the parking lot. Andi watched as he started the four-wheel-drive vehicle and pulled out onto the road. She returned to her notes and tried to concentrate on the work at hand, but was unable to give it her undivided attention. Her thoughts kept turning to Jim, an uneasy combination of her suspicions about him mixed with the very real sensation of the sensual earthiness of his kiss from the day before.

She was not supposed to check back with Steve Westerfall until the next morning, but she needed to seize the opportunity of Jim's absence and make the call. She hoped Steve had been able to gather some information in the short time she had given him. She slipped on her jacket and snow boots and hurried to the office to make her call.

"Do you have anything for me yet?"

"I don't know what you've stumbled into, Andi...." Steve's voice sounded too serious. She recognized the tone, it was the one he used when he knew something was amiss but had not figured out exactly what it was…yet. "But be careful. Jim Richards has been an employee there for the past four years. Prior to that…" He paused a moment.

"Yeah? Prior to that—what?" Her anxiety traveled the phone lines loud and clear.

"Prior to that there is no record of this guy ever existing, either in Canada or in the States. It's a cold, dead trail. Keep in touch, Andi. In fact, I think it would be a good idea if you phoned me every day."

Her voice was anything but enthusiastic. "Sure, Steve, if you think it's necessary. And thanks for the information."

A hard knot twisted in the pit of her stomach. There could be several explanations. Maybe Steve had made a mistake; after all, she had not given him much time. As much as she would have liked to believe that, she knew it probably was not true. Steve was very thorough in his work. If he had felt the information was inconclusive or possibly suspect, he would have said so.

That left only one plausible explanation. Jim Richards had created a false identity and tucked himself away in this remote location because he was hiding from something or someone. The question now was, *Why* had he chosen to hide away behind a false identity? She stepped out of the office and glanced at her watch. It had been almost an hour since he left for the village. She looked toward his cabin, then again to the parking lot. She made her decision.

Her hand trembled slightly as she turned the doorknob. She was not sure if she was pleased or unhappy when she found the door to his cabin unlocked. She took one more look toward the parking lot, then quickly entered his cabin, closing the door behind her.

He had told her that he did a lot of reading, but she had not expected anything like the sight that greeted her. Books and magazines everywhere—not strewn around in clutter, but neatly placed on the bookshelves that lined all the available wall space in the living room. There was a book on the end table next to the couch. A slight smile curled the corners of her mouth. It was the most recent Wayne Gentry mystery.

She wandered around, quickly scanning the shelves, trying to get a fix on his reading tastes. He seemed to read everything: popular fiction, science textbooks, how-to guides.... She allowed that it probably had to do with the isolation of his living circumstances. She noted a television and VCR and next to that a cabinet filled with tapes.

She peeked into his bedroom. The bed was unmade. A pair of sweatpants were draped over the arm of a chair and a pair of socks were on the floor. As in the living room, bookshelves lined the walls. She checked the bathroom. A bottle rested on a shelf next to the shower. She picked it up and studied it for a moment, her brow furrowing in confusion. It was a bottle of color shampoo in a medium brown. Why would he have shampoo that put color into his hair? He did not seem old enough to have gray hair. He did not strike her as the vain type, either. So why would someone who lived alone in the middle of nowhere even worry about it?

She returned to the main room. There were some books stacked in a corner, books that seemed to be somehow separate from the vast array of those lined up on the shelves. Her gaze became glued to the words on the covers. They were chemistry books. She picked up one of them.

A gust of cold wind swept across the room. A chill moved up her spine and her mouth went dry. Her heart pounded hard in her chest. She knew the chill was from more than the cold air. A sick feeling churned in the pit of her stomach as she slowly turned around.

Chapter Three

Jim stood framed in the opened door. His impassive features formed an expressionless mask across his face. His eyes, however, flashed a hint of the conflicting emotions hidden inside him—a conflict that she could not read. His voice was very controlled giving no hint as to what was beneath the surface. "Were you looking for something specific or just browsing?"

"Jim...I, uh..." She was unable to get out any coherent words.

"Yes?" He stepped into the room and closed the door. "You were what?" He heard the edge in his voice, an edge he did not like. It was an anxiety that betrayed the uneasiness he tried desperately to hide. His alert gaze darted around the room, trying to determine exactly what she had been doing.

"You...uh..." She swallowed, trying to remove the lump from her throat. "You said you read a lot. I was wondering if you had any reference books that I might borrow." She knew it was a feeble lie.

"What type of reference books? You thought I just might have some light reading material about toxic waste?"

She stared intently at him. Again, something around

the eyes, his nose, the shape of his face. Her anxieties were doing internal battle with her instincts. She glanced at the chemistry books again and thought about the bottle of hair color. She knew the answers she sought were staring at her, almost yelling at her, but she could not quite make all the pieces fit together.

She desperately wanted to leave his cabin, to lock herself safely inside her own cabin and try to put some sense and logic to all of this. "I...I'm sorry about this. I had no right to barge in here without asking. So...if you'll excuse me, I'll return—"

"Not so fast, *Miss Sinclair.*" He moved toward her, his size suddenly looming even larger than he really was. He reached her in three long strides and grabbed her arm to prevent her from trying to leave. "Exactly what are you doing inside my cabin?" He tried to quell the fear that seemed to be controlling his actions. "What are you looking for?" He was only vaguely aware of how tight a grip he had on her arm.

She searched the intensity of his eyes, trying to read his mood, trying to calculate the severity of her predicament. This was not the first time she had been in a dilemma that could go either way as far as danger was concerned. Her year in investigative reporting had given her enough experiences to be in one of her own books.

He studied her for a long moment, not quite sure what to do or how to proceed. "Who are you? Andrea Sinclair, winter guest at an out-of-the-way summer resort? Wayne Gentry, writer of mystery novels? Or perhaps a stranger who has just invaded the privacy of my home in search of..." He cocked his head and studied her again. He was not sure what he was seeing. It appeared to be a combination of apprehension, guilt and maybe a little hint of panic, but it was not fear. "In search of what?"

She swallowed hard. Other than his grasp on her arm, she felt nothing threatening from him. He appeared to be suffering as much from jangled nerves as she was. With her free hand she tugged at his fingers, trying to loosen his grip. Her voice held an unwelcome husky quaver as she spoke. "You...you're hurting me."

The air swirled with the combined stress and tension each was experiencing at that moment.

He maintained his strong hold on her arm but did loosen his grip a little. He tried to convince himself that things were all right, that there was nothing to really worry about. She had not answered his question. "Why did you come here? I don't mean that story about writer's block, I mean how did you pick this particular place?"

"I...I didn't pick it. In fact, I had never heard of it. My agent chose it." The thud of her heartbeat reverberated in her ears. It was not fear, at least not fear of Jim. She recognized the signs of her own confusion beginning to come together into some sort of cohesive reality. "He had stayed here a few summers ago and thought it would be a good place with no distractions." She saw the uncertainty in his eyes, the wariness.

After a long pause he released her from his grasp. "What's your agent's name? I want to look it up in the records."

Andi rubbed the spot where his fingers had squeezed into her arm as she took a couple of steps back from him. The situation was growing more bizarre by the moment. The circumstances, by all manner of logic, should have created an intense feeling of dread in her, a real concern for her own safety. Oddly enough, that was not what had happened.

She had run a gamut of emotions, but fear had not been one of them. She maintained eye contact with him. In total defiance of all things rational, she felt the mesmerizing pull of his presence, the tingling sensations of excitement she had experienced when he had kissed her. Her voice quavered slightly as she tried to project a calm, controlled demeanor. "My agent's name is Keith Martin of Martin Literary Associates in New York." She saw the quick flicker of recognition dart through his eyes.

Keith Martin—of course. That had been the first summer Jim had been at the resort. It was Keith Martin who had suggested he try the Wayne Gentry novels. He had forgotten the name until she had just mentioned it. A sigh of resignation escaped his lips as he leaned back against the end of the sofa and folded his arms across his chest.

His voice was calm, the tone soft yet conveying the fact that he had regained emotional control of the situation and of his anxiety. "That brings us back to my original question. What are you doing in my cabin? What exactly are you looking for?"

A strange feeling of inner calm settled over her nerves. His body language told her he was in no way threatening her. She relaxed her tensed muscles, quickly making her decision about how to answer his question—how much truth to reveal. She chose her words carefully, trying to put as much sincerity into them as she could.

"The truth is…I was wondering about you. I'm a mystery writer. To me it's a bit of a mystery why someone would choose to lead such a solitary life. It seemed to me that it would be very lonely for you. I meant no harm, I only wanted to satisfy my curiosity about what type of surroundings you had chosen for yourself— how you spent your time.'' She offered him a tentative smile as she gestured toward the walls lined with bookshelves. ''I see what you mean about reading a lot.''

He was doing an excellent job of hiding whatever was going on inside him. She saw nothing in his expression nor anything reflected in his hazel eyes. She adopted what she hoped would appear as a confident persona and moved toward the door. ''Again, I apologize for trespassing. It was very rude of me. I'll leave you to your work and I'll return to mine.''

Jim rose to his feet and hastily moved toward the door, arriving there before she did. He put his hand on the doorknob, preventing her from opening the door. His voice was low, his tone ominous. ''Not so fast, Andi.''

A little shiver of anxiety darted through her as he blocked her way. She tried to sound casual as she spoke. ''Yes?'' She looked into his eyes and saw his uncertainty.

''There's more going on here than just that.'' He was instantly sorry that he had said anything. At that precise moment he was not at all sure he really wanted to know what was going on inside her head.

She lowered her gaze, breaking eye contact with him. There was an awkward moment of silence, then he stepped aside and opened the door. Without looking at him, she quickly left his cabin.

Jim watched her through his window as she hurried across the open area toward her cabin. He knew there was no way he could simply ignore the situation and hope it would go away. He had to determine how much of a threat Andrea Sinclair was to him—indeed, to his very life—and what he needed to do about it. He turned away from the window, his heart heavy with his sorrow.

Andi entered her cabin and closed the door, anxious to get out of sight from his prying eyes. Things were very confused, very unsettled. A small seed of an idea, almost an errant thought, had taken root in the back of her mind—a thought so ludicrous that it almost caused her to laugh out loud at the absurdity. Coincidence was one thing, but this was too much.

With trembling fingers she withdrew the yellowed newspaper clippings from their large envelope and shuffled through them until she found the news photo. She stared at it for a long moment before picking up a pencil and carefully sketching in a beard and a mustache, then lengthening and darkening the hair. She placed the pencil on the table. Her mouth went dry and her legs felt weak. She stared at the altered news photo of James Hollander and saw Jim Richards staring back at her. The man whose life and whereabouts had become almost an obsession for her was the very same man whose sensual kiss had set her soul on fire and still lingered in the heated depths of her consciousness.

Excitement replaced Andi's shock as it raced through her like an out-of-control wildfire. In retrospect she now realized that all the signs had pointed in this direction—his original reaction to her research, his subtle but insistent questions, even the chemistry books in his cabin. Everything made sense now.

Suddenly she felt the panic he must have experienced when he heard of her research. She vividly recalled the expression on his face when he had read the crumpled piece of paper he had picked up from the floor. What must his life have been like these past five years? What had made him choose to disappear like that? So many questions...did she dare to confront him with the knowledge that she now knew his true identity? What would he do if he knew she was on to him? A desperate man feeling trapped...was she truly in danger?

The loud knock on her cabin door startled her into the here and now. It could only be one person. Her nerve endings itched with uncertainty, and a hint of queasiness churned in the bottom of her stomach. He had allowed her to leave his cabin earlier. Had he since had misgivings about that decision?

The voice came from the other side of the closed door. "Andi...answer me. I know you're in there." He again pounded his hand on the door. "There's a phone call for you in the office."

A phone call? That certainly was not what she had expected. She answered him without opening the door. "A call for me?"

"Yes. It's Keith Martin calling from New York. He says it's important."

"In the office? Thank you. I'll get my coat and be right there." She cautiously opened the door and peered outside. She did not see him anywhere. She glanced toward his cabin, then hurried up the path to the office.

Andi grabbed the receiver that rested across the top of the phone. "Hello."

"Andi...it's Keith. Are you all right?"

"Why, yes...shouldn't I be?" Her confusion was obvious. She could not imagine what had prompted Keith's call.

"Are you alone?" His voice sounded urgent. She did not like the signals it sent out.

"Yes. What's the trouble?"

"That's my question. What I have are two unrelated incidents that, when put together, smell like a lot of trouble. First was a call from your buddy, Steve, asking me what you were working on, and then someone broke into my offices and the only thing taken was my file on Wayne Gentry…including your name and address in La Jolla. I wouldn't have made any connection normally, but with Steve's call I'm wondering if this could have something to do with your publisher issuing a press release about your next book being based on the Buchanan Chemicals' case."

Her pulse jumped as the full impact of his words hit her. "My publisher put out a publicity blurb about what I've been researching? How could they?" She tried to slow down her sudden increase in heartbeat and calm her rising panic. Suddenly everything was swirling around her completely out of control, not the least of which was her accidental discovery of the long-missing James Hollander. Could it all somehow be related—her research and the break-in at Keith's office?

"There's nothing unusual about them doing that. You're a hot commodity, so they're just capitalizing on a little free publicity. Most of my clients are thrilled when the publisher gives their potential sales a boost with free publicity." There was a pause before Keith continued, his concern clearly conveyed in his voice. "Andi…sometimes you take too many chances, push things just a little too far. Are you getting in over your head? Are you into something dangerous again?"

"I…" She was not sure how to answer him. She tempered her excitement with caution, not wanting to blurt out the information about James Hollander. "I don't know, Keith. I've stumbled onto something so bizarre that even I'm not sure it's real." She again paused, a sudden decision having popped into her head. "I'll be going home tomorrow. I'll call and make my reservations right now."

"You call me as soon as you get home. Better yet, call me from the airport before you get on the plane. Steve wouldn't tell me why you contacted him, but whatever it was it has him concerned."

Andi forced a casual chuckle. "You know Steve. He's a worrier. That's what makes him so good at his job. He worries about all the little details."

Keith's voice was stern. "Don't fluff me off, Andi. This sounds very serious. If you're in danger—"

"I promise to call from the airport tomorrow. Now I've got to make reservations for the car ferry from Victoria to Seattle, change my flight from Seattle back to San Diego, and let the rental car company know that I'll be bringing their car back a lot earlier than scheduled. And after all that I still have packing to do."

Jim carefully replaced the receiver on the phone extension in his cabin. A little twinge of guilt passed through him. He had always respected other people's privacy and would not, under normal circumstances, even consider listening in on someone else's phone conversation. The circumstances, however, were anything but normal.

Things were beginning to fall into place, to make sense. All of this really was a cruel quirk of fate. If there was, as Keith Martin had said, a publicity release about the subject of her next book, then the break-in at his office and the theft of her file could only be the work of some of the thugs who worked for Milo Buchanan. Subtlety was not one of their attributes, and the government agents would not have been so obvious about their actions. Jim's heavy sigh of resignation only confirmed what he already suspected—Milo Buchanan had not given up trying to track him down.

Jim allowed himself one tiny glimmer of comfort—at least Andi appeared to be exactly who she said she was and had not told Keith about her obvious suspicions. He left the relative security of his cabin, knowing she was still in the office taking care of the changes in her travel plans. It would provide him the opportunity he needed. He quickly covered the distance between his cabin and hers. Every minute was crucial.

As soon as he entered her cabin he spotted all the news clippings spread out on the table. His gaze became riveted to the altered news photo. There was no doubt in his mind that she knew exactly who he was. A band tightened across his chest as the tension mounted inside him. This was not a game, it was literally a matter of life and death to him. He had to know her intentions.

He waited inside her cabin door, standing to one side of the front window so that he was not visible from outside. He watched as she left the office and started back up the pathway.

A minute later Andi burst into the cabin, shrugging out of her jacket as she kicked the door shut behind her. The break-in at Keith's office upset her far more than she had let him know. Things were getting out of hand. She needed to pack and get out of there as quickly as possible.

A sound grabbed her attention. She whirled around and saw Jim standing by the window. His intense stare bored right through her. A startled gasp sprang from her throat as her hand flew to her mouth. Her pulse raced so fast she could feel it throbbing. She searched his face, then his eyes for any sign of his intentions. She did not see anger, but she did see a great deal of pain and uncertainty. She watched as he walked to the table and picked up the altered news photo and held it out toward her. "No more games, Andi. You've obviously figured everything out."

She finally found her voice, the hard lump in her throat making it difficult for her to speak. "What do you intend to do to me?"

"Do to you?" He wrinkled his brow in confusion and slowly shook his head as if he did not quite understand why she would ask such a question. "What makes you think I intend to do anything to you?" He took a calming breath as he plopped down on the couch. He leaned back and closed his eyes. His face looked haggard and drawn.

His voice held all the weariness of someone who had reached the end and no longer had the energy to fight. "Who have you told about this? Do I have time to pack my things and disappear into the night or am I out of time and out of luck, with the final inevitability just outside that door?"

This was a far cry from what she would have envisioned had she been able to project the circumstances. This was certainly not the way the characters in her books would have behaved given the same situation. But then, this was not fiction—it was real life. He was not someone she had created out of her imagination. He was a real person and apparently in very real trouble.

Andi studied him for a moment before responding to his question. It had almost seemed to her as if he was relieved to have everything out in the open, that he did not need to pretend any longer. "Jim..." She gently touched his arm. "I wasn't sure myself until just a little while ago. Every instinct told me things were not what they appeared to be, but I had no idea what the truth was. In my wildest flights of imagination I never could have dreamed up this scene." She paused a moment before continuing, trying to read what was going on inside him. "I haven't told anyone, but there's—"

"Andi—" He turned his entire body toward her. His whole manner came alive as he aggressively grabbed her shoulders in his strong grip. His alert gaze quickly scanned her features, then settled on her eyes. Distress blanketed his features. "You mentioned the second attempt on his—" The words caught in his throat as a bittersweet smile played with the corners of his mouth. "Correction—the second attempt on *my* life." He regained his momentarily assuaged intensity. "How did you know about that?"

His words caught her totally off guard. She blurted out her answer, surprised at the nature of his question. "It was on one of my interview tapes. Why?"

He felt his eyes widen in shock, the same shock that flashed through his body like a bolt of lightning. "You interviewed someone who mentioned the second attempt on my life? Who? I've got to know, Andi. Who told you about the second attempt?"

His sudden aggressiveness seemed to bewilder her. "I don't remember exactly who it was other than the fact that it was one of the federal agents. I don't recall which agency he worked for. It's on one of the tapes at my house." She shook her head. "I don't understand what's so important—"

"No one knew about it, Andi. Absolutely *no one*. I never reported that second attempt. I've never mentioned it to another living soul."

The realization slammed into her. Panic tried to take hold, forcing her to squirm out of his grasp and jump to her feet. "Jim—Keith said someone broke into his office and stole the file with my name and address."

The shock and confusion completely cleared from her mind. Her thoughts came one after the other with remarkable clarity. "You! Someone thinks I have some kind of information that will lead them to you!" She grabbed his arm and tried to pull him up from the couch. "Come on. We've got to contact the authorities. Once you're safe they can get these guys and put them away."

"No!" He yanked his arm from her grasp. "Don't you understand, Andi? It was someone connected with the case who sold me out to Buchanan. How else could he have known where they were hiding me? That same person is probably still around, and he might not be the only one. There wasn't anyone I could trust then, and there isn't anyone I can trust now. If I turn myself in I'm as good as dead. Until I can identify the person who sold me out and see that he's put away, I'll never be able to see that Buchanan is brought to trial."

"Oh, no! I've put your life in danger." The alarm in her voice said almost as much as her words. "Even though there's nothing at my house or in my research that says I know who or where you are, I'm sure there are several things in my house that say where I went. Anyone desperate enough to break into my agent's office then go to my house would not stop there. They would come here looking for me—and they'd find *you*." She grabbed his hand and again tried to pull him up from the couch. "Come on! We've got to get out of here!"

Her thoughts and realizations were moving at such a fast pace that she was not giving him an opportunity to respond to them. He pulled her back down on the couch, grabbed her by the shoulders and took control of the situation.

"Hold it! There is no *we* in this matter. I'm the one they want. If anyone thought there was any tangible connection between us, then you'd be in real danger."

"There's no time to debate this issue. Let's get packed and get out of here. I have a plane reservation late tomorrow afternoon out of Seattle. We'll get out of here now and drive to Victoria. I made a reservation on the car ferry to Seattle and then—" Suddenly a new thought hit her. "No, wait a minute. Anyone who traced me here in hopes of finding you would surely have the airports covered."

She pursed her lips for a moment as she thought about what she had just said, then her manner brightened. "We'll drive all the way. No one would be looking for a couple traveling by car all the way from Canada to San Diego."

He studied her for a minute. It was an odd turn of events. She was actually talking about the two of them leaving together. If things were not so deadly serious it would almost have been amusing, the strange way the circumstances had changed. An odd sense of calm settled over him. It felt so good to have someone to talk to, someone to be around without constantly having his guard up while hiding behind a facade. Trust was a luxury he could no longer afford. Did he dare take a chance on her, or was it just wishful thinking?

"Andi...be reasonable. You can't get yourself

mixed up with this." He moved his hands from her shoulders to her face, framing her loveliness as he studied her features. "You can't get mixed up with me. You don't have a clue as to what you'd be letting yourself in for." His voice was soft with just a touch of sadness. "This is no kind of a life for anyone...least of all a beautiful, intelligent woman with an exciting future ahead of her."

She maintained eye contact with him for a long moment. "As to what I'd be letting myself in for...I might as well tell you the truth right now because you'll soon find it out." She saw the anxiety come into his eyes, felt the tremor move through his hands. "I'm a very stubborn woman and will not be put off by silly platitudes. Even though it was totally unintentional, the fact is that I am involved and I cannot snap my fingers and suddenly make it not so."

His expression was stern and his manner commanding. A new look of skepticism covered his face. "I don't understand your attitude. What's in this for you? Is an accurate ending for your book more important to you than your own safety?"

He had to talk some sense into her, make her understand just how dangerous the situation was. "Listen to me, Andi. One woman is already dead because of me. Do you understand that? Dead—not a little bit hurt or merely frightened. I'm talking blown up by a car bomb. Stone-cold dead. I refuse to put anyone else in a position where it could happen again." He pulled her closer. "Especially you."

His expression softened a little, but his command of the situation continued. "I don't think you're in any real danger—at least not yet. You'll check out of here and you'll go home just as if nothing had happened.

Even if someone does go through your house they won't find anything connecting you to me. I can get Jacob from the village to cover me here. He's done it several times before, so there's nothing unusual or suspicious about it. In fact, he's the one who checked you in when you arrived. By the time anyone realizes I'm not coming back, it will be too late. I'll already have disappeared."

His face was very close to hers, their lips almost touching, his voice a mere whisper. "I wish we could have met under different circumstances, at some previous time."

She placed her hands on top of his as they cupped her face. "But we didn't meet under different circumstances. We know each other now and under these—"

Without giving her an opportunity to finish her sentence he lowered his mouth to hers and enveloped her in a kiss that bordered on barely controlled passion.

She slipped her arms around his neck and ran her fingers through his thick hair while returning his kiss, her own heated passion matching every bit of the intensity that radiated from him. She had told him the absolute truth about being stubborn. She had no more intention of letting this story slip through her fingers than she did this man who made her insides quiver like an impressionable schoolgirl's. There was something she had, one of her taped interviews, that held a clue to solving this mess. They would follow up on this lead together.

He pulled back from her all-too-tempting presence, breaking off the delicious kiss that fanned his longing for more of her. As much as he wanted this to continue, time was all-important. His husky voice laid bare his unfulfilled desires. "Thank you for the romp in the snow yesterday. It was the only carefree moment I've had in longer than I can remember.''

Her voice carried a touch of sadness. ''It's not fair. You're not the criminal. You should be able to have all the carefree romps in the snow that you want.''

He quickly brushed his lips against hers again, the moment of sorrow touching him. ''No one ever said life was fair. Now, you have to pack and get out of here and I have some fast decisions to make. First of all, you'll have to look for the name of the person who told you about the second attempt on my life. It's the only solid clue I've come across that could put an end to this nightmare and I don't intend to pass it up. By necessity I have to disappear again, but at least I now have something tangible I can grab hold of...something to keep me going when it looks hopeless.''

He looked longingly at her for another moment. ''I'll try to drop you a postcard from time to time. I'm sorry that I won't be able to let you know exactly where I am or where I'm going, and until this is over I won't be able to see you again. If things were different, then maybe—''

She placed her fingertips against his lips. ''Listen to me. I have influential friends, people who can be trusted. We'll get to the bottom of this...everything will work out.'' She was not sure who was talking, the woman who instinctively knew a hot story when she found one or the woman who had been so involved with this man's life for the past four months that she could not separate her research from the reality of the situation. She did not want to even think about the woman who had been so strongly attracted to this stranger from the first time she met him, even before she knew who he was.

He cradled her head against his shoulder and nestled his cheek into her short auburn curls. "The answer is *no*. I can't let you get involved. You have no idea what you'd be getting yourself into, who you'd be up against. It's much too dangerous."

She shoved herself away from his embrace, her determination saying she considered the matter closed to debate. "I'm already involved. Now, we're wasting time." Her manner was all business. "You'll have to leave your car here. Your Canadian license plates would be too noticeable and make us too easy to spot as we get farther south. Besides, mine is a rental that I picked up at the Seattle airport. I can turn it in when we get to California and trade it for something different with California license plates. That way it will be just another local vehicle on the highway—one indistinguishable from a million others."

He slowly shook his head, his disapproval surrounding every word. "Then what? We get to San Diego and then what?"

Her mind was working almost faster than she could keep up with it. "We get my tapes and you can listen to the interview that mentioned the second attempt. Maybe you'll pick up on some little thing that escaped my notice, a word or comment that didn't mean anything to me. Then we'll check out the person who gave me the information. Before we leave here I'll put in a call to Steve Westerfall and let him in on what's happening."

She saw the expression cross his face as soon as she mentioned involving someone else. But Steve was okay, he had to be let in on it. "It's all right. Steve is one of the most respected investigative—"

"I know who he is. I almost contacted him five years

ago. Maybe if I had…'' His voice trailed off. Idle speculation served no purpose. All the what-ifs in the world would not change things.

''He has thousands of contacts all over the country. He knows just about everyone, and more important, he can be trusted. In fact, I'd trust him with my life.''

He fixed her with a hard stare. Perhaps she had not intended it that way, but her words were truly prophetic. ''That's exactly what you'd be doing, trusting him with your life. Do you really want to take that kind of a chance?''

Chapter Four

Until now there had not been a glimmer of hope, but with the interview tape Andi had, maybe…just maybe. Jim brushed his fingertips across her cheek as a sigh escaped his lips. Was he desperately grasping at straws?

Her response was all business and put an end to any further discussion of the matter. "We're wasting time."

Jim reluctantly followed her across the compound to the office where the pay phone was located. He still was not convinced that he was doing the right thing in agreeing to involve someone else, but Andi seemed to be a force of her own who refused to take no for an answer. He stood by as she placed her call.

She quickly explained to Steve Westerfall about her accidental discovery and what she and Jim planned to do.

"Andi, are you crazy?" Steve's disapproval shouted across the phone line. "You should have contacted me immediately when you realized he was the missing witness without letting him know you were on to him. You're lucky he didn't relegate *you* to the land of the permanently missing."

"He's not like that. He's a very nice man who desperately wants all of this to be over so he can lead a normal life again. Now, I told you about the second attempt on his life. That was the reason for his disappearance. Without Jim's testimony, the government can't hope to get at Buchanan. Someone on the government payroll sold Jim out. He had to go into hiding to protect himself until the day that he could discover who Buchanan had bought off—there's just no other way to figure it."

Steve's audible sigh said he still was not completely satisfied. "All right. I'll start a background check on everyone involved with the case, particularly those who had access to the protective custody procedures and the witness files. There's one more thing, Andi. I don't want you communicating with Keith Martin. There's a possibility that his office and his phone may have been bugged in addition to the file being stolen."

He paused briefly before continuing. "I'm sure this line is okay for the moment. I called Keith, he didn't call me, and, as usual, he didn't mention my last name."

Steve's voice took on all the attributes of a general giving orders to his troops as he issued instructions to Andi. "Get out of there as quickly as you can. You remember the system we used while working on the Radcliff exposé?"

"Yes."

"That's what we'll use on this."

Nothing more was said. The line went dead as they both disconnected from the call. She silently berated herself for her carelessness. She had been away from the day-to-day reality of investigative reporting for too long. The thought of someone else being aware of

Keith's phone call had not occurred to her. Now she was truly worried.

She turned toward Jim. "We've got to get out of here right *now*."

The urgency in her voice said it all. He instinctively knew there was no time for discussion or second thoughts. He had to pursue this new lead. He might never have another opportunity like this one.

STEVE WESTERFALL LEANED back in the comfortable easy chair in his den after hanging up from Andi's call. He carefully turned over several things in his mind, formulating a game plan and making decisions. Milo Buchanan...the original case had exploded out of nowhere. James Hollander had opened a can of worms that led all the way to the top of Buchanan Chemicals, right to the head man himself.

The U.S. Attorneys office had been trying to make a case against Buchanan Chemicals. They had gathered bits and pieces, but nothing concrete, nothing that would allow them to actually go after someone as powerful and influential as Milo Buchanan—nothing, that is, until the day James Hollander walked into the Chicago office of the U.S. Attorneys and presented himself to Phil Herman.

When James Hollander disappeared right from under their noses the day before he was to testify, it had blown the case. Phil Herman had dropped all the charges against Milo Buchanan and then had immediately resigned and taken an early retirement. Buchanan had continued with business as usual. Yes, Steve Westerfall was very familiar with the case.

And now, after five years, Steve Westerfall suddenly had verification that the only person who posed a genuine threat to Milo Buchanan was still alive. And even better, he had someone on the inside close to Hollander who could keep track of his every move.

A slight smile curled the corners of Steve's mouth as he reached for one of the special hand-rolled Havana cigars. His wife hated the smell of the cigar smoke and insisted that he not smoke them in the house. But this was definitely a special occasion.

IT WAS LATE THAT NIGHT when Andi and Jim arrived in Victoria. He chose a small motel close to the ferry dock on the inner harbor. Her car trunk was crammed full, not only with her things but with everything of his that would fit, including his chemistry books. If it did not fit into the car, then he had considered it gone forever. He had learned over the past five years not to get attached to anything...or anyone. Andi had given him a bad time about taking up valuable room with the useless chemistry books, but he had been adamant. It was his way of holding on to one little piece of who he was, of who he hoped to be again some day.

He glanced at Andi as they pulled into the motel parking lot. He was still not sure he had made the right decision in agreeing to go along with her plan. If something happened to her because of him, or if she had some sort of hidden agenda of her own... He refused to finish the thought.

Jim smiled graciously at the desk clerk, then signed the register as Mr. and Mrs. Denton from Spokane, Washington. "Perhaps something in the back, you know...something out of the way. Alice and I are still on our honeymoon." He leaned forward and gave the clerk a sly wink as he lowered his voice in a suggestive manner. "We wouldn't want to disturb the other guests."

The clerk gave an appreciative glance toward Andi, then handed him the room key. "Sure thing, Mr. Denton."

Jim drove around behind the motel, parking the car where it could not be seen from the street. He carried the two overnight bags and Andi unlocked the motel room door.

He looked around the small room as he set the bags on the floor next to the closet. "Well, not exactly the lap of luxury." He turned a mischievous grin toward her in an attempt to break through the strain and discomfort of the circumstances. "What do you think, Mrs. Denton? Will it do?"

She felt the embarrassment color her cheeks as her gaze dropped to the floor. "Did you have to tell him that?"

He dismissed his grin and the light manner, once again allowing the seriousness of the task to dictate the terms. "I'm sorry if I embarrassed you. To have asked for separate rooms would have looked very suspicious, even to have asked for two beds..." He felt his own embarrassment try to get a foothold. "Well, anyone looking for you or me wouldn't be looking for a honeymooning..." His words trailed off. The awkwardness of the situation weighed on both of them. Finally he went to the closet and pulled the extra blanket from the top shelf. "I'll sleep in the car."

She took the blanket from him. "You can't do that. It's freezing out there." She looked into his eyes. Her words were soft and contained just a hint of uncertainty. "I'm sure we can be adult about this. After all, a couple of kisses don't automatically mean..." She again lowered her gaze to the floor, her embarrassment taking control. Nothing more was said as each silently prepared for bed.

Andi gathered her things and disappeared behind the bathroom door. When she finished, he took his turn. As soon as he was out of sight she took off her robe and climbed into bed, pulling the covers up around her shoulders. Jim reappeared from the bathroom about ten minutes later.

He stood on the other side of the bed dressed only in a pair of gray sweatpants. She tried not to stare, but could not help taking in his well-toned torso—his strong arms, his hard chest and flat belly. An involuntary shudder moved through her body when she saw the ugly scars low on his chest and across his right side, the results of the car bomb. She tried to ignore the desire she felt while averting her eyes as he settled his body into the other side of the bed.

FRANK NORTON READ the publicity release about the forthcoming Wayne Gentry novel with great interest. Even though there had not been any activity on the Buchanan case in the past few years, it was still an open file for him. When Phil Herman immediately dropped all charges against Milo Buchanan, then just as quickly resigned his position following the sudden disappearance of James Hollander, Frank Norton had managed to step up from Assistant U.S. Attorney in the Chicago office to take over Phil Herman's job.

Even though there had been no mention of James Hollander's whereabouts for at least two years—not even a false report or dead-end lead—Frank Norton still wanted to locate the missing witness even if it was nothing more than being able to confirm his death. He did not like loose ends, and that's exactly what James Hollander and the open case file represented. He had aspirations toward the governor's office, and closing this particular file would look very good on his record.

And equally as important to Frank Norton was the fact that it would allow him the glory that had escaped his predecessor. Phil Herman had been the primary obstacle to his goals, but when he resigned under a cloud of disgrace over the missing witness and his failure to prosecute Milo Buchanan, it left that door wide open for the younger and more ambitious Norton.

He needed to find out what, if anything, this Wayne Gentry had found out about the missing James Hollander, if possible without going the subpoena route to get Gentry's research material. A writer would probably attempt to stand behind the same rights that the press claimed with regard to protecting sources and material. He needed to keep a very low profile on this. The last thing he wanted was for his actions to become public knowledge before he had everything in place. But prior to delving into this new bit of information, he had a more important phone call to make.

He dialed the number of the Chicago office of the U.S. Marshals. "Sally? It's Frank Norton. How have you been?"

Sally Hanover's surprise at the identity of her caller was evident in her voice. "Frank? Well, it's been a long time...at least a year. What's up?"

Sally and Frank had first met a little over six years ago. They had dated casually for a couple of years, but the relationship never had any serious overtones and had finally faded away. Yes, Sally was definitely surprised by Frank Norton's call.

"Just touching base with an old friend. I thought we

might have dinner. How does your schedule look for this week?''

"Well...maybe I could work it out tonight. To tell you truthfully..." Sally's hesitation had a very disconcerting affect on Frank, a definite roadblock to his plans. "I've been seeing someone else."

"Are you still dating...oh, what was his name? The flashy kid with the FBI who was involved with us on the Buchanan case."

"You mean Cliff Turner?"

"Yes—that's the one. I never did understand how an FBI agent could afford that Rolex watch and the Porsche that he drove."

Sally's voice became defensive. "He inherited a lot of money from his...well, I think it was his grandfather—" her voice trailed off a bit as it took on a hint of doubt "—or was it his uncle." She regained her assertiveness. "Well, anyway—he said he had inherited it from some relative."

Frank chuckled good-naturedly, although it sounded a bit forced. "Sorry, I didn't mean for that to come out as an accusation. It was just an observation. So, how about dinner?"

"I'm seeing someone else right now—not Cliff—on a pretty regular basis. He's a man I started doing some freelance computer work for and...well, we've sort of developed a relationship."

"I'd still like to take you to dinner tonight, if you're free. Just a couple of old friends enjoying a meal. I'm sure this man couldn't have any objection to that. Do you want to get back to me after you check with him to see if it's okay?" It was a calculated comment on Frank's part and it elicited the hoped-for result.

"I don't need to ask anyone's permission. I'm perfectly capable of making my own decisions. I'm free for dinner tonight.''

"That's great, Sally. Why don't I pick you up at your office at five-thirty? Is that too early?''

"No, that should be just about right. I'm getting ready to run a computer search right now that will take me most of the day."

"You always were the best computer expert the department ever had. In fact, there might be a little job you could do for me, strictly confidential. We can talk about it over dinner. I'll see you this evening." Frank placed the phone receiver in the cradle, very pleased with himself.

JIM GLANCED AT HIS WATCH. It was almost six-thirty in the morning. He had been up for half an hour and had already taken a shower. He leaned back in the chair and stretched his long legs out in front of him. Andi was still asleep. He laced his fingers together, then leaned his chin against them as he studied her. Only her head peeked out from under the blankets. Her hair rested in disarray across her cheek and forehead. Her face seemed free of any worry. She looked as if she did not have a care in the world.

He did not know if she had fallen asleep immediately or had lain awake as he had, afraid to move. As much as he had wanted to hold her in his arms, to share the long-denied closeness of another human being, he knew it could not happen.

Jim glanced at his watch again, then quietly rose from the chair and grabbed his jacket. He stole one more lingering look at her, then silently slipped out the door as she turned over on her side and snuggled comfortably under the blankets.

Andi slowly became aware of being awake. She did not move, preferring instead to allow her mind to drift. It had been such a strange sensation, being in bed with a man and pretending that he was not there. She wondered if Jim had felt as ill at ease as she had with the unusual circumstances.

She did not know what time it was when she had finally fallen asleep, but it seemed as if she had stayed awake for quite a while. Such strange thoughts had gone through her mind. One moment she wished he would wrap his arms around her and kiss her with the same intensity as he had when they were back at the cabin, and the next moment she was afraid that he just might try to do it.

That was not the only thing on Andi's mind as she lay in bed, quietly savoring the first moments of being awake. She knew Jim was committed to following up on the lead she had unwittingly provided. However, she was not at all sure just how committed he was to her continued involvement in his quest. She could see it in his eyes, hear an occasional hint of it in his tone of voice. Once they reached her house and he listened to the tape, would he disappear again? She shoved the disturbing thought from her mind as she turned over and opened her eyes.

Andi sat bolt upright, all her senses instantly alert. Jim was not in bed, not in the room. She looked toward the bathroom. The door was open and the light off. He was nowhere to be found. She jumped out of bed in a panic and raced to the window. She shoved the curtain aside and pressed her forehead and nose against the pane. Her warm breath created a foggy screen on the cold glass. A sigh of relief was her response when she spotted the car still parked where they had left it. But where was Jim? Had he waited for her to fall asleep, then quietly slipped away from her, never to be seen again?

She grabbed her robe and headed for the bathroom, emerging ten minutes later after a quick shower. She threw on some clothes and ran a brush through her hair. As she reached for the door it swung open and Jim entered the room, pulling the key from the lock.

"Where have you been?" Her demanding shout came out as a combination of panic and irritation.

He leveled a cool look at her and held up the paper sack he had in his hand. "I found us some coffee. I had to go two blocks away to a restaurant. It was too early to get coffee at the motel office, it wasn't ready yet."

"Oh…" She glanced down at the floor, unable to hold his gaze. "I…I thought you had—"

"Changed my mind? Taken off in the middle of the night while you were asleep?"

Her voice softened. "Something like that." She studied the pattern in the worn carpeting, too embarrassed to look him in the eye.

He paused for a moment before answering her concerns and fears. "Don't think it didn't occur to me. It was touch and go there for a while."

She finally looked up at him, into the intensity of his hazel eyes. "Then why did you decide to stay?"

Again, who was asking the question? Was it the woman who wanted an ending for her book about James Hollander, the missing witness, or was it the woman who wanted more of Jim Hollander, the man?

"This is never going to end unless I make it end. The interview you have on tape is the first solid clue I've had in five years. If I let this opportunity pass by, then I might as well walk into Milo Buchanan's office and tell him he's won. Like it or not, I have no choice but to go along with you—'' his pointed words left no confusion about his meaning ''—for now.'' He reached into the sack and withdrew a cup of coffee and handed it to her.

''What then?'' The question frightened her. ''After you've listened to the tape, are you as good as gone?''

''I...I don't know.'' A discernible sadness clung to his words. ''I no longer make plans any further into the future than a day or so.'' He removed the lid from the paper cup and took a sip of the hot coffee. The silence weighed heavily in the air for a moment, then each turned to packing the few belongings they had brought into the motel room.

There were so many things to do before the ferry sailed. In an attempt to further obscure their travels they had decided to take a different car ferry, crossing Juan de Fuca Strait directly south to Port Angeles, Washington, rather than down Puget Sound to Seattle.

After breakfast they went to the currency exchange by the Empress Hotel. Not wanting to take a chance on a bank account, over the past four years Jim had accumulated several thousand dollars in cash that he kept in his cabin. He handed five hundred dollars to Andi and took out five hundred dollars for himself. The stress began to weigh on him. Every person he passed on the street looked suspicious. More than once he whirled around to see if the person he has just passed had turned back to watch him. He sent Andi into the currency exchange ahead of him while he anxiously waited outside until the other customers had gone.

Finally the time arrived to board the ferry. They each felt the nervous tension churn just beneath the outer calm. They decided to go separately as if each were traveling alone. Andi drove on board and Jim walked on as a foot passenger. The ninety-five minutes it took to get from Victoria to Port Angeles put their arrival shortly after twelve noon. It was nearly one o'clock before they finally headed out of town.

She could see it on his face and feel it in the very air that surrounded them. She tried to imagine what he must be going through at that moment, the highs and lows he was experiencing, but she could only guess. As much as she wanted to, she was not able to put herself in his place. He would periodically glance over toward her, as if he were seeking reassurance that this was the best course of action. She would offer him her most confident smile, but he would just return his attention to the road without making comment, his eyes constantly scanning the surrounding area and the occupants of any and all cars within his line of sight.

The next few hours passed without incident. She told him all about herself—her family background, her education, her career, starting with her year working for Steve Westerfall. She even told him about Nick, the real reason she had been having trouble concentrating on her book. She wanted him to know as much about her as possible, wanted to do whatever she could to relieve the tension that she knew must be building layer upon layer inside him, and make him feel more comfortable about the fact that she knew his true identity.

She tried to explain how and why she had decided to use him as the central focus for a book. "And then I decided to go through my clipping file. I found four different articles that I thought would make the basis for an interesting book. I finally narrowed it down to one—the Buchanan Chemicals case."

"So that's how I was lucky enough to have you stumble across me and my little problem—I was a clipping in a file folder."

It was the first thing he had said in more than two hours, and the sarcasm was unmistakable even though the words were uttered without enthusiasm. But at least he had finally said something.

She attempted to maintain an upbeat attitude in spite of his glum disposition. "Yes, it was one little clipping about a missing government witness. It was only a couple of paragraphs, but it got me thinking. That's when I decided to see what I could find out about the case and the witness. And the rest, as they say, is history."

When he did not respond, she tried again to draw him into conversation. "Well, those are pretty much the highlights of my life. What about you?"

"I'd say you already know everything there is to know about me. I don't know what else I could add."

He felt trapped. Every few minutes he sneaked a quick glance in the sideview mirror to see what vehicles were behind them. As much as he needed to hear her tape and find the name of the person who told her about the second attempt on his life, he wanted to be out of the car. He was not sure exactly why. Was he uncomfortable with the personal closeness that had developed between them in spite of his efforts to curb his desires? Or was it that nagging concern about trust and whether he should once again put his fate into someone else's hands?

From Port Angeles, Andi had driven south, connecting with Interstate 5 at Olympia, Washington. Her intention was to stay on Interstate 5 all the way to San Diego. It would be the quickest and most direct route. He had adamantly insisted that they stay off the obvious freeway and stick to the coast, taking Highway 101 all the way south. It would definitely add time to their schedule, but he said he felt more comfortable with it.

The disagreement was settled abruptly, accompanied by a heated exchange of words. He had taken over the driving chores when they stopped in Portland, Oregon, to buy gas and had simply ignored the interstate and her plans, choosing to follow the Columbia River over to the coast. It was late when they stopped for dinner, then checked into a small motel in Astoria, Oregon, at the mouth of the Columbia River.

"You know this is going to cost us another day." Andi slammed her overnight bag down on the bed, making no effort to hide her anger as she glared at him. "If we'd stayed on the interstate we would already be in California and could have been at my house by late tomorrow night, but now it's going to take us two more days. We won't even talk about the storm clouds that have been with us all day. Rain will cost us even more time on the winding coastal route."

His anger matched hers, his voice getting louder. "Haven't you ever heard of that tried-and-true expression, better safe than sorry?"

She could not stop her heated words as she continued to glare at him. "That's not exactly right. Rather than being a tried-and-true expression, it's a tired old cliché that has nothing to do with this!" She stood her ground, her hands on her hips and her scowl riveted on him. "This isn't tourist season with lots of strangers invading the towns along the coast. We're much more likely to stand out in some small out-of-the-way place rather than being one car among thousands on the—"

Without warning he grabbed her arm and pulled her body hard against his. His mouth captured hers with a

demanding intensity. And she responded to that demand with the same fervor as he demonstrated. He
wound his fingers in her soft hair, his actions the cul-
mination of his released anger meshing with his pent-
up desires and frustrations.

He felt the situation slipping out of his control. He
had not expected her response to be so evenly matched
to his own desires, despite their previously shared
kisses. He was not sure what he was experiencing. It
had been such a long time since he had been able to
talk and act without carefully monitoring each word
and action in order to protect his identity. He did know
one thing for sure. This incendiary moment had to stop,
and had to stop now before it was too late. He reluctantly broke off the kiss.

Her insides trembled with every quaking breath she
drew. Nowhere in her research notes about James Hollander was there anything that prepared her for the type
of raw sexuality that reached out and grabbed her.
Never in her life had anyone ever made her feel that
way—and it scared her right down to her toes.

He took a calming breath, his voice soft but in control. "Do you have any idea what you've done to my
life? You've taken a situation that, with the passage of
time, was finally becoming tolerable to me and you've
turned it inside out. You've shoved me right back into
the harsh glare of the public eye—maybe not at this
moment, but with the publication of your book everything would be wide open again."

He took another steadying breath. "You're also the
first person I've been able to talk openly with in five
years. This is a horrendous amount of change to have
to adjust to in such a short amount of time, especially

considering what's at stake here—" his voice trailed off for a moment "—at least for me."

He snapped back to attention, his manner becoming more authoritative as he sharply clipped his words. "You want me to trust you? Then you're just going to have to humor me and my little whims or paranoia, whichever you choose to call them."

Things were becoming too complicated. She could—

Chapter Five

Neither could deny nor question the reality of the emotional tie that bound them together. It was a tie constructed of a much more complicated substance than merely needing to get to her house so he could find and follow a lead that would hopefully release him from his exile. Things were becoming much more involved than that.

Her voice was a whisper that carried just a hint of huskiness. "I have to find a pay phone. I need to check in with Steve."

He held her an instant longer, then finally loosened his grip and allowed her to step free. His mind turned to more practical matters. Should he go with her? Listen to what she was telling Steve? Trust was something he had not indulged in for a long time. It was not easy to resurrect the feeling without serious reservations regardless of how much he wanted to. He pondered the question a moment longer before responding. "I saw a pay phone next door at the gas station."

"I'll be right back." She turned and left the room, closing the door behind her.

Andi hurried next door, found the phone, inserted the coins and dialed the number. The call was answered with a sharp beep from Steve's pager. She punched in the number of the pay phone, then hung up and waited. She knew Steve would immediately go to a pay phone and return her call rather than taking a chance on making the call from his home phone.

Things were becoming too complicated. She was allowing her personal feelings and emotions to become too tightly entwined with the business at hand. It was a cardinal rule, one that Steve had carefully pounded into her head—*never* become personally involved with someone connected to an investigation. It clouded the judgment, and if the stakes were high enough could ultimately cost someone's life. She knew she was blazing an extremely foolish trail, especially considering the very real danger that already surrounded him…and now her. His words came back to her. *One woman is dead.*

Five minutes later the phone rang. She grabbed it on the first ring. "Hello."

Steve did not address her by name and did not use his own name. He did not need to ask where she was, he would simply cross-reference the phone number he had called. "Is everything okay?"

"Yes, so far. It looks like we'll be an additional day getting to my place. He's very uptight and on edge. We had a disagreement about the route and I lost."

There was a moment of silence before Steve responded to this new information. "I don't like it, but I guess there's nothing that can be done about it right now. I've got a new computer wiz working with me. I think she can hack her way into anything. Of course, her regular job puts her in a position to already have access to quite a bit of information. I should have more to give you next time you call."

The conversation lasted less than thirty seconds. Andi glanced at her watch as she left the phone booth. It was late and they needed to get an early start in the morning. A little shiver darted through her as she wondered what the night would bring. Could she spend another night in the same bed with Jim and still be able to ignore the way he turned her senses upside down?

Jim watched out the window as Andi left the phone booth and started across the parking lot from the gas station back to the motel. Very mixed emotions churned in the pit of his stomach. When she went to use the phone, he had almost run after her so he could hear exactly what she said to Steve. He needed the information she had in her possession. It was an impossible situation. He was bound to her by the circumstances as surely as if they were handcuffed together.

He quickly undressed except for his briefs and climbed under the covers. He lay on his back, the covers pulled to his waist and his hands behind his head. If he was lucky maybe he would be able to fall asleep in the next minute before she returned. It was either that or else he would have to seriously consider sleeping in the car. To spend one more night in the same bed without being able to at least hold her was asking too much of the tenuous grasp he had on his self-control. His thoughts were interrupted when Andi entered the room.

She removed her jacket as she filled him in on her conversation. She pointedly avoided looking at him. "Steve's been very busy. He should have quite a bit of background information on several of the people involved in the case by the time we get to my house."

"Did he say anything else?"

"There's not a lot that can be said in thirty seconds.

I'll talk to him again tomorrow when we stop for the night.''

He noticed her uneasiness, the way her eyes glanced away. He could not tell if she was keeping something from him, perhaps some information Steve had given her, or if it was as simple as her feeling as awkward about the sleeping arrangements as he did.

She quickly unpacked her things and went into the bathroom. He snapped off the lamp on the nightstand and turned on his side, facing away from the bathroom door. He closed his eyes and tried to force away the tension building in his body. He heard the bathroom door open, felt her weight come down on the bed as she slipped under the covers. He took a calming breath, then turned over to face her.

"Andi…" He hesitated a moment, then enfolded her in his arms and held her against his body while cradling her head against his shoulder.

Her voice quavered slightly. She had wished he would take her in his arms just as much as she had not wanted him to take that initiative. "Jim…this isn't—"

"This is all, Andi. I'm not asking for more." He made no further advances, he only held her.

He wondered about the future. For the first time since this unending nightmare had begun, he actually thought about what the future could be, then the dark cloud of doubt covered his thoughts. Was he allowing his mind to drift beyond what was possible? Exactly what was Andi's angle in becoming involved? What did she have to gain from this? Was she someone who could really be trusted or did she have some kind of ulterior motive? Exactly what had she and Steve talked about?

"MR. BUCHANAN." Gordon Conklin's voice was all business as he entered the office. Even though it was late at night, Milo Buchanan was still at his desk. "After a thorough search, we got all of Andrea Sinclair's research material out of her house. We found out that she's gone to Canada...some little place on Vancouver Island. There's nothing in her house that says she knows Hollander or even knows where he is, but this sure is a funny time of year to be headed into Canada to some little summer resort in the woods. Do you want me to send someone there to check?"

The phone rang, interrupting their conversation. Milo Buchanan picked up the receiver, listened for a moment, then spoke rapidly. "Hold on, I'll be with you in a moment."

Milo pushed the hold button then placed the receiver in the cradle. He returned his attention to Gordon. "Yes, Gordon, I want you to send someone there. I don't want the slightest thing overlooked. Every possibility should be followed up and explored to the fullest. Now, if you'll excuse me, I have other business to tend to."

He leaned back in his chair and watched as Gordon left the office. As soon as the door was closed, he lifted the receiver and released the hold. "Now, just what is it that you think I'll find so interesting?"

MILO BUCHANAN WAS NOT the only one receiving a late-night call. Phil Herman had just turned out the lamp next to his bed when the phone rang. He may have resigned his position as U.S. Attorney following the Hollander disappearance, but he had continued to keep on top of any and all information concerning the

Buchanan case and in particular the possible whereabouts of James Hollander.

"Hello"

"Phil, it's Steve. Sorry to be calling so late."

"I'd given up on you for the night. I'd just gone to
bed. I take it you heard from her?"

"Yes, we just got off the phone. Things seem to be
progressing, but a little behind schedule. He's being
difficult and she's frustrated by it. It seems to be a
matter of control. He wants to call the shots, but as
long as she holds the trump card of the interview tape
he isn't in a position to really make his demands stick.
I'm sure he's as frustrated by everything as she is."

"Do you foresee any problems in him going along
with her?"

Steve paused for a moment before responding to
Phil's question. "No, I don't think so. She has something he wants, and sticking with her is the only way
he can get it. I don't think we need to worry. Andi can
handle him."

There was a note of warning in Phil's voice. "Are
you sure? I don't need to remind you what's at stake
here. James Hollander has managed to successfully
evade any and all attempts to find him for five years.
If this blows up on us and we lose him before we can
get everything set up, there won't be another chance."

ANDI LAY QUIETLY IN BED the next morning, still
wrapped in Jim's arms as he slept. She listened to the
sounds outside the window. The noises from the busy
harbor on the Columbia River mingled with the roar of
the early-morning city traffic. She also heard the sound
of rain falling hard against the roof, the windows and
the pavement outside the motel room. It was not a good

omen. The rain would slow down their travel time. She allowed a quick twinge of anger—it was another reason why they should be on the interstate rather than the narrow, winding coastal highway.

She glanced at Jim's face, then slowly raised her hand and touched his cheek. She gently scratched her fingers through his beard, quickly withdrawing her hand as he began to stir. He brought his hand out from under the covers and swatted at her fingers, as if he were shooing away a fly. She noted how the color of his hair and beard had lightened a little with his last shower.

Her voice was a whisper. "Do you really like having this beard? You'd be much more attractive without it."

His words held the thickness of sleep. "It's been sort of a necessity, like dying my hair. I've never particularly liked it." He shifted his weight slightly while tucking his arm back under the covers, still not opening his eyes and not relinquishing the hold he had on her with his other arm. "What time is it?"

"It's a little after seven and it's raining out." Her entire body felt alive, her senses tingling in response to his touch.

"We'll get up in a little bit. I just want to stay here awhile longer. It's warm, it's comfortable—" he slid his hand across her back, feeling the soft material of her nightshirt "—and it's a closeness I haven't felt in five years." His words became tinged with just a hint of melancholy, his mind now fully awake. "Maybe even longer." As with the spontaneous romp in the snow, she had once again provided him with a glimpse of what life would be like if he could only put a stop to the insanity that stalked him.

She had felt it, too—the closeness, the warmth. She

remained quiet for a few minutes longer, then gently pulled away from his embrace. "This rain will slow us down, we have to get on the road."

Andi gathered a few belongings, then disappeared into the bathroom. As soon as she finished Jim took his turn.

When he emerged from the bathroom, the beard and mustache were gone and some more of the brown color had been washed from his naturally blond hair. Two or three more washings with regular shampoo and most of the brown would be eliminated. She allowed a slight grin to turn the corners of her mouth.

He smiled at her. "Well, what do you think? Do I stick out like a sore thumb?"

His handsomely chiseled features captured her total attention. "You didn't do that on my account, did you?"

"No, not exactly. I never did really like it, and since you already know who I am, this seemed like a good time to get rid of it." He allowed a serious expression to cross his face. "Besides, if anyone shows up at the resort, the only description they'll get of me will be of a man with brown hair and a beard and mustache."

They headed south along the coast. The rain was steady, not falling hard enough to be a downpour but definitely more than just a shower. Andi glanced over at Jim as he drove. He seemed more relaxed than he had the day before, his face showed less tension, and he did not have as tight a grip on the steering wheel. But he could not hide the fact that he was troubled by something. Andi's thoughts turned once again to what would happen after they arrived at her house and he had listened to the tape.

Travel was slow, the other cars taking their time on

the rain-slicked, winding road. She had started to say something about being on the interstate but changed her mind, not wanting to cause another argument. Once they left Oregon and entered California, Highway 101 would be fine. They could stop at the airport in Eureka, California, and turn in the Washington rental car and pick up a California one. She glanced at her watch. With the slow time they were making, Eureka would probably be their stop for the night.

She tried to get him to talk about himself, about what he had been doing the past five years. He did not respond to her gentle prodding. He had made an attempt at some polite conversation, but she could tell that it was a very shallow effort and probably nothing more than a means of evading her questions.

The rain pounded down harder as the morning turned into afternoon. He had lapsed into silence as he gave his complete attention to the slick, winding road and the slow traffic. It was already getting dark when they passed through Brookings, Oregon, just a few miles from the California state line. With the rain, the darkness and another one hundred and fifteen miles to go— all but the last few miles of it still two lane winding highway—she knew it would take them close to three hours to get into Eureka.

Even though they had shared the driving chores, it had still been a long, exhausting day for both of them. Finally they reached the spot where the highway widened and straightened out, where they were able to drive at maximum highway speed. Not only was Andi tired but she was also hungry. They had elected to keep driving rather than taking the time to stop for dinner. She stifled a yawn.

He squinted as he peered through the windshield at

the road ahead, the headlights barely penetrating the rain that was now coming down in sheets. They continued on in silence, the back-and-forth swishing of the windshield wipers and the tires on the wet pavement the only sounds.

There was more on his mind than just the rain and the difficult driving conditions, more than his concern about her subtle attempts to delve into what he referred to as his *missing years*. He could understand her natural curiosity, especially in light of her research, but that did not mean he needed to roll over like a puppy who wanted his tummy scratched. Regardless of how much he wanted to cross over the line into the realm of trust, all he could muster was a marginal step forward—just enough to be in a car driving south toward La Jolla— and he was not comfortable with even that. He could not shake the almost overwhelming feeling of trepidation that burrowed in the pit of his stomach.

"There!" Jim pointed to some lights up ahead. "A motel set back off the road and right next to a pizza place. How about that?"

Her weariness, a result of the late hour and the long day, showed in her voice. "Anything is okay with me, and I'm definitely hungry."

Jim dashed through the rain to the motel office while Andi waited in the car. A few minutes later he returned and drove around to the back of the motel. They parked beneath an overhang from the roof, quickly gathered their overnight bags and went to the room.

"I've got to check in with Steve. It's very late, especially in New York. He's going to be worried."

It was well after midnight in New York when she placed the call to Steve from the pay phone at the pizza place next door. Following her conversation, she joined

Jim at the table. They ate quickly. It seemed to Andi that it was raining even harder as they dashed back to the motel, sidestepping large puddles as they ran. Occasional flashes of lightning lit up the black sky, followed by loud claps of thunder.

She grabbed her overnight bag and disappeared into the bathroom, emerging a few minutes later wearing her robe over her nightshirt. He had taken off his shirt and kicked off his shoes but was still wearing his jeans. The air crackled with electricity, then there did not seem to be any air at all as they stood on opposite sides of the bed looking at each other.

Jim finally found his voice but was not happy with the way it sounded. "This was the only room they had, otherwise I would have gotten two rooms...or at least a room with two beds." He glanced around the room. "I'll sleep in the chair."

"You can't do that. That chair is too small. You won't be able to get any sleep." It was a strange scene unfolding in her mind. Her body tingled with the sexually charged atmosphere that filled the space between them.

His words were thick, and an edge of huskiness crept into his voice. "I'll get more sleep in that chair than I will in that bed trying to keep my hands off you."

She knew cooler heads should prevail, which was the exact tone he was trying to project. She knew the importance of what they needed to accomplish should be enough incentive to keep things under control. She also knew that her desires were quickly overtaking her logic.

She glanced at the chair. "I'd be more comfortable in the chair than you would. I'll sleep there...or maybe on the floor." She went to the closet and retrieved the extra blanket, then took one of the pillows from the bed.

He took the blanket and pillow from her hand and went to the large chair in the corner. He settled his large frame into the chair, pulled the blanket up over his shoulders and closed his eyes. "Good night, Andi. I'll see you in the morning."

She climbed into bed and turned out the lamp. "Good night, Jim." She lay awake for a long time, listening to the intensity of the storm and trying to sort out things in her head. She had always prided herself on her levelheadedness and clear thinking, but for the past few days she had been very confused about her feelings. She knew this man so well, yet did not know him at all.

She had wanted, with all her heart, for him to make love to her. But it could not happen. She also knew Steve was correct about personal involvement complicating things far more than they already were. As Steve had told her when they spoke earlier, he had put the plan into motion and it was too late to change things now. She could not allow personal feelings to jeopardize what needed to be done. She finally slipped into a light sleep.

She did not know how long she had been sleeping when the sound of the storm roused her to wakefulness. She lay on her side, staring blankly at the window, watching as the lightning lit up the outside for an instant, only to disappear and then be followed by the sound of thunder. Then another flash illuminated the surrounding area.

Andi's heart jumped into her throat. There, just outside the window, the silhouette of a person. She sat up, all her senses alert as the adrenaline surge pumped through her body. Was Jim awake? She listened but did not hear anything other than the storm. Another flash and again she saw the silhouette against the window.

She slipped out of bed and made her way across the room toward the chair, the rush of fear lingering like the rumbling of the thunder. Her voice may have been a whisper, but the urgency was implicit. "Jim—are you awake?" She reached out and grabbed his arm, shaking him as she spoke. "Jim...there's someone standing outside the window."

He jerked to attention, turning toward the direction of her voice. His words may have been thick with sleep, but his senses were fully alert. "What? Where?"

"Outside the window...there's someone there. You can see the silhouette each time the lightning flashes. Look—" It took only a moment before another flash revealed the silhouette to Jim.

A cold tremor of fear sliced through his body. Someone had found them, somehow they had been followed. Whoever it was had waited until they were asleep and the noise of the storm would cover any extraneous sounds. He moved swiftly, his words a hushed whisper as he searched for his shoes. "You get some clothes on. I'll open the door and rush him. You get yourself around the corner of the building as fast as you can and find someplace safe to hide."

She knew there was no time to argue with him or challenge his orders. This was his area of expertise, not hers. He was the one who had successfully evaded several government agencies and Buchanan's people for five years. She pulled on her jeans and jammed her bare feet into her boots. He listened for a minute at the door, then flung it open. The cold, wet wind bit into his face just as another flash of lightning lit up the scene.

"Hey, you!" Jim's voice carried above the sound of the storm. "Get out of there!" He grabbed Andi's arm, preventing her from leaving. He had been momentarily stunned at the sight that greeted him—someone wearing a rain poncho attempting to break into the car. A car thief—a common, run-of-the-mill car thief.

The thief's head jerked up and turned toward the sound of the shout. Jim saw that it was a teenage boy. The boy quickly took off running around the corner of the building and out of sight. Jim closed the door, snapping on the light as he turned toward Andi. His voice contained the relief he felt. "Well, my heartbeat has almost returned to normal. How about yours?"

"Not quite yet." She took a calming breath. "I'm not sure it'll ever be normal again."

He put his arm reassuringly around her shoulder, his voice soft without negating the seriousness of his words. "Now do you see what I mean? How getting yourself involved in this nightmare is no life for you? How the slightest little thing can send the adrenaline pumping through your body?" He turned her until she faced him. "Are you sure you want to continue with this insanity?"

She rested her head against his shoulder. "Yes, I'm sure. I have something at my house that will help you put a stop to this so you'll be able to put Milo Buchanan away and begin to lead a normal life again." She looked up into his face, into the concern in his eyes. "How can I not continue with this?"

Her question remained unanswered as Jim glanced at his watch. "It's five-thirty. It'll be daylight by the time we get ready and hit the road."

"We need to go to the Eureka airport and turn in my rental car and get another one before we head out of town. If the weather doesn't slow us down and if we luck out on the traffic through San Francisco and Los Angeles, it'll still be nine-thirty or ten o'clock tonight before we get to La Jolla—and that's an awful lot of ifs." She reached up and touched his cheek, feeling the stubble of his overnight whisker growth. "It'll be a very long day."

Both of them moved quickly, and they were soon on their way to the airport and the rental car agency. She approached the only clerk on duty, her voice filled with confidence.

"I'd like to turn in this Seattle rental and get another one." She handed him the paperwork and smiled.

The clerk looked at her suspiciously, then studied the rental contract. "Let's see, you rented this at SeaTac airport almost two weeks ago, indicating that you would be returning the car to the same location, then you drove here and now you want to exchange the car for another one?"

She looked at him, her eyes widening in perfect innocence. "Is there a problem with that?"

"Well, no. It's just that it's a rather unusual request. Where will you be returning the exchange vehicle?"

"We'll turn it in at the rental office at the San Diego airport." She noticed the look in the clerk's eye as he studied her for a moment, then turned his attention toward Jim.

Jim leaned toward her and snuggled his face into her hair, partly to conceal it from the clerk and partly to play out the charade they had planned should things not go quickly and smoothly. His words were whispered but said loud enough for the clerk to hear.

"Come on, honey. We need to be on our way if we're going to get to that secluded little seaside inn by lunchtime. And then we'll have the entire afternoon—just the two of us, a bottle of champagne, the sound of the rain, the hot tub and the king-size bed...." He allowed his voice to trail off, having said enough for the clerk to get the idea.

Andi glanced shyly at the clerk and offered an embarrassed explanation. "We were married in Washington but decided that rather than flying back to San Diego we'd drive along the coast and take our time. We'd like to exchange the car for a van, because we want to stop in wine country at some of the antique shops. A van will give us the room to take our purchases home with us." She breathed an inward sigh of relief as she saw the acceptance in the clerk's eyes and the slightly lascivious grin on his lips.

"You're in luck. I happen to have a very nice van that's ready to go. We'll just take care of this paperwork and then you can be on your way."

Chapter Six

Frank Norton paced nervously up and down his living room floor. He should have been on his way to his office half an hour ago. Finally the phone rang, the call he had been waiting for. "Where the hell have you been? You were supposed to have called an hour ago. I have office hours to maintain, I can't spend my mornings at home waiting around for phone calls."

"So stop wasting time by complaining. What's so urgent that we couldn't take care of it in your office?"

Frank's voice had an obvious nervous timbre to it. "I don't want this to reach the wrong ears, and there's no way I can be one hundred percent sure that my office is completely secure regardless of what they tell me."

"So, what's the problem?"

"It's Ross Durant. He's been acting very suspiciously the last couple of days. I've had no less than four phone calls from him. He doesn't really say anything, but with each call he sounds more stressed-out than in the one before. There's definitely something going on with him and I don't like it. I think you should have someone look into it. He's due for retirement in a couple of years. If Ross has decided that his government pension plus his other investments aren't enough and has changed allegiance, then we need to know about it. We also need to know how long it's been going on. In fact, there are a couple of other people whose names have popped into my mind the past day or so in connection with Hollander."

"Oh? Who did you have in mind?"

Frank tried to swallow his nervousness. "Lou Quincy, for one. He was head of the U.S. Marshals office here in Chicago. As I recall, he was unhappy about his lack of career advancement. He and Phil Herman were about the same age. They used to commiserate about having to live on a government pension in the very near future. We need to find out what the hell is Ross Durant's problem and confirm what Lou Quincy has been doing lately. I've already started making some discreet inquiries along those lines. The possible repercussions from this won't be pretty, especially if it gets into the press."

"That's all you're worried about? I'll have my people check on Ross Durant and you look into Lou Quincy's activities. Try to do it without making it seem like an official inquiry."

"I can take care of my end, you just make sure you don't do something that will cause any adverse publicity. I don't want anything standing between me and the governor's office." Frank replaced the receiver in the cradle and left for his office.

THE RAIN WAS AS HEAVY as it had been the night before as Jim and Andi drove south out of Eureka, the only saving grace being that it was now daylight. They made small talk, but it was obvious that they each had things on their minds, things they were not talking about.

Andi cautiously approached a situation that she knew was going to cause an argument, but it had to be brought up before they got to her house. She nervously cleared her throat as she thought over the exact words she would use. "There was something else when I was talking to Steve last night...." She did not like the uneasiness that had settled in the pit of her stomach or the less-than-firm tone of her voice. She knew Jim well enough to know he was not going to like what she was about to say. "He has an informant who might be willing to meet with me—"

"You!" The shock of her words caught him totally off guard. He snapped his head toward her, momentarily taking his attention from the road. An edge of anger crept into his voice. "What the hell do you mean by *meet with you?* This is my problem, not yours. If anyone meets with an informant it's going to be me, not you."

Even though it was the reaction she had expected, her irritation at his overbearing response pushed her anger to match his. "It's my lead, I'm the one who's meeting with him. If you show your face before it's safe then we could blow this whole thing—"

"Your *lead?* You think this is a competition of some sort to see who wins the plum assignment?" He jerked the van to the side of the road, the tires squealing as he braked to a halt. He twisted around in the seat until he faced her. He saw the defiance in her eyes and the stubborn set of her jaw. He would show her that he was equally determined. "I'm telling you—"

"You're *telling* me?" Her voice became louder as her anger rose. "You mean you're giving me orders? Who do you think you are?"

His words were emphatic without being loud. His

subdued voice held a strange calm that bordered on ominous. "You want to know who I think I am? I think I'm the man whose entire life has been turned inside out, who has lived a hellish nightmare from the moment I discovered what Milo Buchanan was up to, who was betrayed by the very people who were supposed to be protecting me. I'm the man who has been on the run for the past five years. And *I'm* the one who will be putting an end to this. If there is a lead to follow or an informant to meet with, then *I'm* the one who will do it—not you."

"You can't meet with an informant if I don't tell you who he is and where the meeting is set to take place."

They glared at each other; the only sound intruding into their heated argument was the rain beating on the roof of the van and the swishing of the windshield wipers.

Her manner softened a little. They still had many hours of driving ahead of them. It was going to be a very long day and they did not have the luxury of wasting time parked on the side of the highway arguing. "We can talk about it when we get to my house."

He put the transmission in gear and eased the van back onto the highway. "There's nothing to discuss. It's going to be done my way." He stared straight ahead, his jaw set in a tight line.

Andi held her temper and her words. Jim's attitude told her there was no use in continuing the argument, at least not at that time. She tried to put herself in his position, to understand what was going on inside him, but she knew she would never really be able to fully understand what he had been through. They continued on down the highway in silence.

What seemed like hundreds of thoughts darted around in Jim's head as he frantically tried to pull everything together. It had all happened so suddenly. Beyond the need for him to hear the interview tape she had at her house, there had been no real plan. Before they even arrived in La Jolla, things had escalated and the stakes had become higher. The information about Steve Westerfall having an informant and Andi insisting on meeting with him said that some sort of cohesive plan had to be determined. It also said that Steve Westerfall and Andi were involved in this much deeper than he had been led to believe. Exactly what had been going on behind his back? It was a concern that lodged in his consciousness and refused to go away. It gave him very mixed feelings about Andi and her true objectives.

He thought about the night before, about the moment he had made the decision to sleep in the chair. There was no way, regardless of how honorable his intentions might have been, that he could have spent another night in the same bed with her without their making love. It was not just that he had been alone for so long—it was Andi. She excited him in a way he had almost forgotten was possible. But could he really trust her? He wanted to, but there were still too many unanswered questions where she was concerned, and the number of those questions seemed to be growing.

Neither of them said much as the miles gave way and the time passed. They finally stopped for a quick lunch in Santa Rosa, about an hour or so north of San Francisco. Andi took her turn behind the wheel when they got under way again. The rain continued, but it had slacked off from the downpour of that morning to a steady rainfall. Jim had remained withdrawn and uncommunicative.

She wanted to turn inland to Interstate 5, where it would be a straight shot right down the middle of the state all the way to San Diego. It was the route she had originally wanted to take. At the town of Novato she turned off Highway 101 and picked up Highway 37 headed east.

Jim sat up straight and looked around, trying to get his bearings. "What are you doing?"

"I'm bypassing the traffic on the city streets through San Francisco. This road skirts the north end of the bay and puts us on the east side." She glanced at him for a moment, then continued. "From there we can cut over to Interstate 5. It will save us two or three hours."

His voice held a sharp edge to it. "I thought we discussed—"

"*We* didn't discuss anything!" Her level of anger matched his exactly. "You were driving so you did what you wanted without regard to the most expedient route. Well, now I'm driving. My way will be quicker, more direct."

He glanced over at her again. They should not be snapping at each other. It could very well be that their time together would be limited to only another day or two. When they arrived at her house and he listened to the tape—

"*Look out!*" He saw the dark form of a large truck cut right in front of them, spewing mud and water across the windshield.

Andi slammed on the brakes. She gripped the steering wheel so tightly that her knuckles turned white as she tried to steer clear of the reckless driver. She fought to maintain control of the skidding van, but the wet road presented too much of an obstacle. They finally came to rest after sliding through the mud onto the shoulder. She took a deep breath in an attempt to force some calm to her reality.

Jim's words came out in a rush as he unbuckled his seat belt and reached for her. Whatever anger had existed only a couple of minutes earlier had disappeared in a heartbeat. "Andi—are you all right? You're not hurt, are you?" He slid over next to her, putting his arm around her shoulder and drawing her close to him.

"I'm fine." Her voice quavered slightly. She took another deep breath to calm her frazzled nerves. "How about you?"

"Yeah..." His voice trailed off as he peered through the windshield, the mud having been rinsed off by the steady rainfall. "It was almost as if that driver had purposely—"

Her head jerked up, her eyes widened in shock. "Do you mean...do you think it was something other than just a reckless driver?"

His voice sounded vague, not at all convincing. "I'm sure it wasn't anything more than a simple accident. The driver's vision was probably blocked by the rain and he didn't realize how close he was."

Jim held her a moment longer before finally releasing her. "I guess I'd better see if I can get us out of the mud. I hope we're not stuck here." He pulled on his jacket and opened the door, squinting toward the rainy sky as he turned the collar up around his neck.

They did everything they could think of to get out of the mud. "Okay—try it again!" Jim put his shoulder against the back of the van and tried to dig his feet in for a more secure footing as Andi pressed on the gas pedal. The tires spun in the gooey mess, spattering mud across the front of his wet clothes, but the van refused to budge. On what was normally a fairly busy road, very few cars had come by during the hour that they had been struggling with the stuck vehicle, and none had stopped to offer any help.

Andi was watching in the side mirror when she saw the highway patrol car pull over behind them. Tremors of anxiety darted around inside her stomach. A reckless driver who may not have been merely a reckless driver and now a highway patrolman who may or may not recognize Jim. She tried to calm her trepidation.

Andi took her foot off the gas pedal, causing Jim to straighten up and look around. Between the rain and the sound of the van motor, he had not heard the car pull up behind him. The sight of the patrol car and the officer opening the door startled him. A twinge of uneasiness tried to take hold, but he shoved it back into hiding as he turned to greet the officer.

The young patrolman approached Jim, pulling his rain slicker up around his neck and placing his cap on his head. His expression was pleasant, nothing to cause any alarm. "You seem to have a little problem here."

Jim carefully measured his words, not wanting to project his uneasiness. "Yes, we've been trying for an hour to get out of the mud, only I think it's worse now than when we first skidded off the road."

"What happened?"

"A truck cut into our lane right in front of us. We had to swerve to avoid being hit and ended up in the mud."

"I'll call a tow truck for you...get you pulled out."

Jim flashed the officer a grateful smile. "Thanks. You're the only person who's bothered to stop to see if we even needed help."

"I'll make that call right now. Should be someone here soon. Where are you headed?"

Jim paused for a moment before answering as he decided exactly what he should say. "We were headed for Sacramento."

"Well, be careful on these roads, sir. There's been a rash of minor accidents due to the rain. I'd also suggest that you get out of those wet clothes as soon as possible before you end up with the flu."

"A good suggestion, officer. Thanks for your help." Jim climbed in the van, keeping a watchful eye on the highway patrolman as he called for a tow truck, then pulled back on the road and continued with his patrol route.

"What was that about?" Andi could hear the tension in her voice. She had been on the edge of her seat from the moment the patrol car had pulled up behind them.

"Everything's okay. He called for a tow truck and said to watch it on the roads." He stared at her for a moment. An edge of irritation crept back into his voice. "Of course, this never would have happened if we had stayed on—"

"I don't want to hear any 'I told you so' speeches! If we'd stayed on the interstate at Portland like I wanted to, we'd be in San Diego by now." She folded her arms across her chest, sat back in the seat and stared straight ahead, her face set in a frozen mask, indicating that, as far as she was concerned, the conversation was over. They remained silent for another hour while they waited for the tow truck.

Jim rummaged through his suitcase, pulled out a dry sweatshirt and sweatpants, and changed in the back of the van. He felt a little better but was still in need of a good hot shower. Another couple of hours and they would lose the winter daylight. It was obvious that they were not going to make it to San Diego, and that meant one more night in a motel together. It was not what he wanted.

He turned toward her, reached out and brushed his fingertips against her cheek, startling her out of her thoughts. "Andi...look, uh...I'm sorry I snapped."

He said what she had wanted to say, what she should have said. "Me, too. I'm sorry for the way I've been—"

He leaned his face into hers, capturing her mouth with a soft kiss. She felt her insides quiver and turn to mush as he twined his fingers in her hair and pulled her to him. There it was again, the unmistakable pull of his sexual magnetism. His kiss was warm, soft and gentle and she did not want it to end.

After several seconds he pulled his face back from hers. He traced the outline of her upper lip with his index finger. His voice was slightly husky. "Things are stressful enough as it is. Let's not argue anymore, okay?"

The honking of a horn broke the magic of the moment—the tow truck had arrived. Within half an hour they had been pulled free of the mud and were on their way again. Andi headed the van inland from the Bay Area until they connected with the interstate. Their conversation became more casual, more relaxed. Jim made no further comments about the route Andi had chosen. Instead he turned his attention to more important matters.

"Tell me more about this informant of Steve's."

"I don't really know very much. Steve said he'd fill me in later. He just said that one of his contacts had been in touch with someone who had a vital piece of information that he was willing to sell.''

''Did he say what kind of information or who the informant was?''

''No, that was all he said.''

They stopped at a fast-food takeout to grab a quick bite to eat. As they stood in line waiting for their food, Andi surveyed the people inside, some sitting at tables and others at the counter placing their orders. Two men in particular caught her attention. They had been standing just outside the door, looking in through the glass as if they were searching for something...or someone. A little shiver of trepidation shot across her skin when they came inside and sat at a table without placing an order for food.

She leaned over and nudged Jim. Her voice was just above a whisper. ''Those two men at that door. Is it just my imagination or do they seem to be—''

''Staring at us?'' The tension had been building inside him from the moment he had spotted the two men. ''Yeah, I saw them standing outside.'' Before he could say anything, two women walked in and joined the men at their table. They appeared to be discussing food, then the two men went to the counter to place an order.

A quick feeling of relief settled inside Jim. He wondered if there would ever be a time when something as simple as two men meeting their dates would not set his senses on edge. He scrutinized the situation a moment longer before offering an opinion. When he was fairly certain that there was no danger, he flashed her a teasing little grin, attempting to keep the situation light.

''I can't imagine why they'd be staring. Just because I've got mud in my hair, all over my shoes and just about everywhere that I have skin showing? That doesn't seem like much of a reason.''

She emitted a little chuckle. ''I guess you're right. It just seemed odd—'' Their order number was called, so they quickly collected their food and left. They ate in the van, then Andi made her call to Steve.

As soon as she returned, she filled him in on what Steve had to say. ''He's flying out tomorrow. He'll be on the first flight out of JFK in the morning. With the time difference, that will put him in Los Angeles about nine or nine-thirty tomorrow morning. He plans to rent a car and drive down to La Jolla from there. He'll be at my house before we are.''

Jim sat in silence for a moment, his jaw clenched in a hard line as he digested this new piece of information. The reticence in his voice told of his apprehension. ''Why is he coming out here?''

''For one thing, he wants to meet you. He's putting a lot on the line and he wants some personal reassurances.''

He looked at her curiously, almost in disbelief, unable to conceal the annoyance that edged into his voice. ''*He's* putting a lot on the line? Tell me, is he putting his life on the line? Is he being expected to trust a total stranger with his life?''

She heard his distress. She understood where it came from, but once again she could not put herself in his place, could not feel what was going on inside him. ''I know this must be very difficult for you.'' She reached over and touched his arm. ''Everything is going to work out just fine. Soon this will all be over and you'll be free again—free to do what you want and go where you want.'' She refused to acknowledge the thought that it also meant he was free to leave and she might never see him again.

"I wish I felt even half as confident about all this as you do."

They rode on in silence for a while longer. It was Jim who finally spoke. "It's getting late and I'm dirty and grubby. If I don't get a shower pretty soon I'll..." He could not stop the chuckle. "I might become short-tempered and irritable."

She laughed along with him, relieved that his mood seemed to have perked up a little bit. "We certainly wouldn't want that, would we? It's still more than eight hours to San Diego. If we get on the road early tomorrow morning we should make it by early afternoon."

It was another fifteen minutes before they found a motel with a vacancy sign. He returned to the van from the check-in office and slid into the passenger seat. He sat quietly for a moment, staring straight ahead, then turned toward her. He held up the single key. "Number eleven. It was the only room they had available."

Neither of them said anything as they carried their overnight bags into the room. The tension was unmistakable, heightened by the sexual energy that filled the air.

Jim was the first to break the silence. "As soon as I get a shower and some clean clothes I'll go out to the van and sleep there. The rain has almost stopped. It's not too cold."

He took a calming breath, then a second one as he tried to quell the desire building inside him—a desire he knew he could not ignore if they were to spend one more night together in the same room. He quickly disappeared behind the closed bathroom door.

Andi heard the shower running. She sat on the edge of the bed, not sure what to do. The circumstances that had brought them together and continued to surround them were anything but normal. If they had stayed on the interstate, they would be at her house by now. There was another truth that was even more compelling, one she had been trying to ignore and Jim had not mentioned. Even with avoiding the Seattle and Vancouver airports, they could have taken a flight out of Portland or San Francisco or Oakland. They could have even taken a commuter flight out of Eureka where they had actually been at the airport to exchange the rental car.

She did not want to explore the probable reason for the actions they each had silently agreed to—actions that transcended the danger surrounding them, the awkwardness of their uneasy alliance and even the importance of what they needed to accomplish.

A few minutes later Jim emerged from the bathroom dressed in clean, dry clothes, his hair still damp from the shower. "I'll be in the van." He paused at her side, cupped her chin in the palm of his hand and lowered his mouth to hers. The kiss was brief, but there was no denying the feelings that had prompted it. He turned and quickly left the room, closing the door behind him.

The rain had finally stopped. Jim pulled open the van door and slumped into the seat. The restless churning in the pit of his stomach refused to calm down. He closed his eyes and tried to compose himself, but it did not work. He left the van and wandered aimlessly across the parking lot as he took stock of his situation. He was away from his safe haven and literally at the mercy of someone who was not much more than a complete stranger, regardless of what lengths Andi had gone to make sure he knew all about her. He also knew that he had no way of knowing if she was telling him the truth.

There had been numerous opportunities for someone to get to him along the route from Vancouver Island. He felt fairly confident that no one was following them, although the moment when they had been run off the road still nagged at his consciousness. He had what seemed like thousands of questions, but no answers. And his biggest question was where and how Andi fit into all of this.

After Jim had left the motel room, Andi took a quick shower and prepared for bed. She fluffed the pillow, then slid in under the cover. She did not know if she was relieved or disappointed that he had chosen to sleep in the van. She suddenly felt very much alone.

The soft knock at the door sent a tremor of anticipation through her body. She quickly jumped out of bed and raced to answer it. He stood on the other side, his handsome features highlighted by the parking lot illumination. His words were soft and hesitant, his manner somewhat awkward as he nervously shifted his weight from one foot to the other. "Andi...I wish I could say I had better control of what's going on inside me, of my hopes...my desires—"

"Perhaps controlling one's desires isn't..." Her voice trailed off; she did not know how to finish her sentence. She stood aside, allowing him to enter the room, then closed the door behind him.

In sharp contrast to the carefully weighed considerations that had always been part of his job as a chemical engineer, snap decisions often based on nothing more than gut instinct had become his way of life. His very existence for the past five years depended on his being able to instantly take in what was going on and make an immediate judgment on a plan of action.

Ever since Andrea Sinclair had entered his life, he had been thrown into a tailspin of indecision. Suddenly other people were making determinations about his life, people he did not even know. It had to stop. He needed to take back control of what was happening to him. The situation of the moment was no different. It would serve no purpose to fence back and forth about what they both knew to be the inevitable.

His voice contained the confidence of a man who had regained control of a tenuous situation, yet it projected a soft quality. "We're both very aware of the strong attraction that's pulling us together, something beyond the outside parameters of this nightmare that's been my life. There's a heat that's barely contained under the surface. I felt it the first time we met."

He placed his hands on her shoulders and searched the depths of her eyes. "I can't make any promises or offer you any type of a commitment. I don't know what tomorrow will bring...."

She reached up and lightly stroked his cheek. "Is this what your life has been like these past five years? No closeness, no emotional involvement, no sharing— carefully avoiding anything that might put you in a vulnerable or compromising position?"

She slipped her arms around his waist and rested her head against his shoulder. "I wanted so badly to get inside your head while I was doing my research, to figure out who you were and what you would be doing. This side of your life never occurred to me." She felt herself being enfolded in the warmth of his embrace as he nestled his cheek against her soft auburn curls. She felt his pain as surely as if it had been her own. She felt the loneliness and isolation that had been forced on him.

"I haven't wanted to be close to anyone…until now. It's too dangerous being around me. I'm not even comfortable with this limited involvement on your part, but no matter what happens in the future I'm very glad that we met." The emotion buried inside him caused his voice to falter. "Maybe some day, if things—"

"No more talk." Her words were whispered as she placed her fingertips against his lips to silence him. "I'm not asking you for any promises. I'm not asking you for a commitment."

Perhaps it was the long hours they had spent together sharing a platonic bed and dangerous secrets. Maybe it was the forbidden enticement of no promises and no commitment. Possibly it was the tenuous present and the uncertain future that caused things to progress as quickly as they had. Whatever the reason, the passion and desire that existed between them seemed far more intense than anything either of them had ever experienced.

A low groan escaped his throat as he seized her mouth with a demanding heat. The immediacy of her response fueled his already-inflamed desires. Their lips met, their tongues meshed, then the tension that had been simmering just below the surface exploded with a force that shocked both of them. The restraint each had been exercising was quickly replaced by the full acceptance of their actions and knowledge of the consequences.

Pieces of clothing quickly fell away. The sound of their breathing filled the air. She placed a trembling hand against his hard chest, his strong heartbeat resonating on her fingertips. She had never before experienced the level of anticipation that surged through her body at that moment.

His lips tickled across her throat, nibbling seductively at the curve between her neck and shoulder. She felt the sensual titillation of his touch as he caressed her shoulders, then slowly slid his hands down her back as he pulled her body tight against his.

She closed her eyes and allowed the exhilaration to wash over her. His touch was magic, his caress gentle yet at the same time insistent. He sank into the bed, pulling her with him. She ran her fingers through his thick blond hair, then wrapped her arms around him. He slowly and sensually propelled her toward the ultimate rhapsody as she savored every step of the exquisite journey.

"Jim...I..." Andi gasped for air. She wanted to say something to him, wanted to share her feelings of the moment but could not force out any words.

The heat of her response and her unbridled passions were addictive—he craved more and more. He wanted to give her pleasure as much as he wanted to take it. He had never met anyone who set him on fire the way she did, who made him totally lose control of any and all reality other than their bodies and souls combined into one. His pace quickened, then his passions boiled over as he gave one last deep thrust. He held her tightly, burying his face in the softness of her hair in order to prevent the words of endearment he feared he was only a breath away from uttering.

He felt drained, but at the same time there existed an excitement and lightness of soul he had never before experienced—certainly not in the past five years. He ran his fingers through her hair, pausing every few seconds to kiss her cheek or forehead while he forced his ragged breathing under control. He wanted to tell her of feelings and emotions that he thought he would never again experience, but he knew he could not, at least not yet. Then his thoughts tinged the moment with sadness—maybe never. There was so much more at stake now than there had been an hour earlier. Not only his freedom, but also any hope for happiness—his entire future.

If everything turned out all right maybe then he could think about the future, a future that included Andi. The next couple of days would tell it all. If the lead of the interview tape and the informant that Steve had uncovered did not work out, then he did not know where else to turn or what else to try. Things just had to work out, especially now that he had found someone who allowed him to have thoughts of a future. He closed his eyes, thoughts of Andi circulating through his conscious mind until he finally fell asleep.

Andi, too, was deep in thought as she quietly reveled in the secure feeling produced by the warmth of his embrace. She had never been as content and happy as she was at that moment. Any thoughts about the truly impossible circumstances that surrounded them were denied admittance, along with the growing realization that she just might be falling in love with him. She snuggled her body against his, her head resting on his chest. The sound of his heartbeat lulled her into a blissful sleep.

Neither of them stirred until the next morning. Andi's movements forced a couple of words from Jim, his voice still thick with sleep. "Good morning."

Andi ran her fingers across his hard chest. "It is a glorious morning, isn't it?" She wrapped her arm across his body and rested her head against his chest.

Her voice became soft, filled with a combination of emotion and concerns. "This situation…these circumstances…everything is so uncertain. Things between us happened so quickly."

He tightened his hold on her, not knowing quite how to respond to what she had said. He was not sure if what he was experiencing was true. "I wish I knew how to put into words exactly what I'm feeling. For five years I've lived my life day-to-day, not allowing myself any thoughts about what the future might hold. Then you came along and gave me hope.…" He could not finish his sentence. Things were far from settled. Everything could fall apart any minute. Buchanan's henchmen could be only a step or two behind him and closing in fast.

She lay cradled in his arms for a quiet moment then sat up in bed, her mind forcing her to deal with more immediate and practical matters. "We need to be on the road."

He placed a soft kiss on her lips. "I know."

Chapter Seven

The nondescript man in his late forties pulled the dark sedan up to the curb in front of the restored turn-of-the-century beachfront bungalow in La Jolla. He sat in the car with the engine idling as he glanced up and down both sides of the street, carefully taking in everything—a man walking his dog along the sidewalk, a woman two doors down mowing her front lawn, the letter carrier delivering the mail, a man reading the water meter at a house across the street and the house next door to that with a For Rent sign in the yard. After a few moments he turned off the engine, got out of the car and quickly walked around the side of the bungalow, pausing long enough to open the gate to the backyard.

Steve Westerfall crossed the lawn, coming to a stop at the back fence. He opened the back gate and stepped out onto the small bluff overlooking the beach. A slight grin tugged at the corners of his mouth as he noticed the new steps leading down to the sand. For the past two years Andi had been telling him that she intended to replace the old weathered steps. His gaze swept the expanse of the Pacific Ocean, then came to rest on the waves that rolled across the sandy beach ten feet below.

It was a beautiful day. The sun shone brightly in the clear blue sky, causing glints of light to dance across the water. He closed his eyes and turned his face toward the warming rays. It had been snowing when he left New York early that morning. He had to admit that it felt good to be in California with the warmth and sunshine, even if his main concern had not been dealing with the emergence of James Hollander from five years of hiding.

A frown momentarily creased his brow. He was also concerned about Andi. It was not so much what she had said but more the way she had said it. He sensed that she was becoming personally involved—emotionally involved. He and Andi went back many years. He genuinely liked her and did not want to see her needlessly hurt. Things were happening very quickly, many more things than he had confided to Andi. He did not want James Hollander to be spooked into running. Now that the elusive Mr. Hollander had finally resurfaced, he needed for him to stay put until all the pieces and all the players were in position. That was Andi's job. The next couple of days would be very critical to his plan.

Steve turned his attention back to the business at hand. He crossed the yard to the patio and was about to reach under the table to retrieve the hidden house key when he saw the broken pane of glass in the French door. He quickly looked around to see if anyone was watching him, then peered through the door into the house. Even with the lace curtain partially obscuring his view, he could tell that someone had broken in and gone through the place. Drawers had been pulled out and the contents scattered on the floor. He hoped he was seeing the work of a common burglar, but his gut instinct told him differently. He quickly returned to his car, making sure he did not touch anything.

He glanced at his watch. It was already one o'clock. If Andi and Jim stuck to the schedule she had outlined for him, they would be arriving within the hour. He grabbed his briefcase from the trunk and slid in behind the steering wheel. He removed a notebook and a cellular phone. A snort of disgust escaped his throat. It had been a stupid and wasted move for them to have broken into her house, obviously in search of information—stupid and desperate. He did allow a hint of a satisfied grin to tug at the corners of his mouth. The more desperate they were, the better it was for him. Desperate moves this early in the game could only lead to costly errors as things became critical.

He dialed a number, and his call was answered on the first ring. "It's me. I'm sitting in front of Andi's house. They aren't here yet, but I have no reason to suspect that things aren't right on schedule. Is everything set up the way we discussed? We're not going to get a second chance at this, so everyone better know exactly what they're supposed to do." He listened for a moment. A hint of irritation crept into his voice. "The money will be there."

He disconnected from that call and immediately placed another one. "I've got a problem. Do you have somebody available for the next few days who can do a little job for me?"

"ANOTHER HALF HOUR and we'll be at my house." The drive had gone quickly for Andi, much more so than she had anticipated. Jim had driven as far as Los

Angeles County, then she had taken over, claiming to be an expert at navigating the tangled web of freeways through the greater Los Angeles metropolitan area.

"You said you live right at the beach?" He reached over and brushed a loose tendril of hair away from her cheek, pausing long enough to gently caress her smooth skin with his fingertips.

"Yep. You walk out my backyard and down the steps and you're on the sand." She allowed a smile that quickly turned into a laugh.

He looked at her quizzically, her infectious laugh causing him to chuckle. "What's so funny?"

"I was just thinking about what you said when we first met, something about why I would abandon the sunny weather of southern California for Vancouver Island in winter. As I look around at this bright, warm day it makes your question even more compelling."

They exited the freeway at La Jolla Village Drive and headed west. It was Jim who broke the silence, his voice carrying a very serious tone. "Pull over for a minute."

She quickly checked the rearview mirror and the side mirror, looking for anything that was out of place. A stab of urgency cut through her. "What's wrong?"

"Nothing's wrong. I just want to say something before we get to your house." He felt the anxiety taking hold again as they approached the moment of truth. Once they were at her house and he had an opportunity to listen to the tape, then things would probably move very quickly. He also knew Steve Westerfall would be waiting for them. It was even possible, as much as he hated the thought, that this might be the last time they would have a chance to be alone together for a while…maybe even forever. He took a calming breath.

Andi pulled the van over to the side of the road, then turned toward him. She tried to smooth the worry lines from his face with her fingertips. "What's wrong, Jim? What's bothering you?"

He took her hand in his and laced their fingers together. "I might not have an opportunity to say this later. I have no idea how all of this is going to turn out or what's in store for me, but I want you to know..." He paused as he tried to focus his train of thought and pull together the proper words. "I want to tell you how very much I appreciate what you're trying to do for me."

He leaned toward her, his mouth capturing hers in a soft, loving kiss. "You're a very special lady, Andrea Sinclair. No matter what happens, I'll always be grateful that fate brought you into my life—" his throat tightened, and he had to force the rest of his words "—even if it's only for a brief while."

"Jim?" Her voice quavered slightly as the uncertainty tried to take hold, "I don't understand. You sound as if—"

She abruptly stopped talking and looked away from him. She sat in silence for a moment, trying to compose her inner turmoil. Steve had been right—don't get involved. It was bad all the way around. She had a job to do and that should be her primary concern, not how this man made her pulse race and turned her emotions inside out.

He leaned back in his seat, staring straight ahead through the windshield. "We'd better be on our way. It's getting late and I'm sure Steve must be waiting for us."

"Yes, I'm sure he is." Andi put the van in gear,

pulled away from the curb and headed straight for her house.

She drove along the quiet side street, her attention constantly darting from one parked car to another as she approached her house. She slowed down even more as her gaze lit on the dark sedan parked at the curb. She spotted Steve sitting behind the wheel talking on his cellular phone while making notes on a small pad. As soon as she was confident that he had seen her, she continued down the block, not altering her speed or drawing undue attention to herself.

Jim had not seen anything out of place, but sensed the change in her behavior and felt the tension level increase dramatically. "Is something wrong?"

"Yes." Andi's voice was calm, but there was a slight edge of apprehension to it. "Steve's sitting in his car instead of in my house. He knows where the key is hidden, and when I drove past he didn't wave for me to stop. He'll meet us in the village in fifteen minutes."

Jim felt the knot tighten in his stomach. For a moment he had held the hope that things would go smoothly, but apparently that was not going to be the case. Obviously Andi and Steve had some sort of pre-arranged signal and meeting place. He remained quiet, allowing her to continue with the plan and nervously waiting to see what would happen next.

Andi drove directly to a neighborhood pub. It was off the beaten path, one of those places where there were only locals and they all knew one another. Any strangers not in the company of a local resident would immediately stand out. They sat in a booth in a quiet corner at the back.

Andi nervously twisted and pulled at the cocktail

napkin underneath her wineglass, methodically shredding it into little pieces. She bit at her lower lip. "I don't like it. I wish Steve would hurry up and get here so we can find out what's wrong."

Jim took a sip of his beer as he watched her. He was every bit as nervous as Andi, even though his outward demeanor seemed composed. But then, he had five years of practice at living behind a facade. He tried to make his voice sound light and teasing as he reached over and touched her cheek. "You're making minced meat out of that napkin." He offered her an encouraging smile as he placed his hand on top of hers. She responded by lacing their fingers together.

Steve had entered the pub and approached their table without either of them being aware of it. He immediately noticed the familiar and intimate gestures between them which only reinforced his suspicions about a personal and close relationship having already developed. His manner was all business as he turned toward Jim and extended his hand. "Jim? I'm Steve Westerfall." The two men shook hands, then Steve sat down.

Jim had never seen Steve Westerfall before, but the man sitting across the table from him was certainly not what he had expected. *Nondescript* was the only word that came to his mind. He appeared to be in his late forties, was average height, average build, average brown hair and eyes. Everything about him was ordinary. He was the type of person you would forget five minutes after meeting him. Jim figured that it was probably that very touch of the ordinary that allowed Steve to be so good at his job.

Andi's anxiety showed on her face and carried over in her voice. "What's going on, Steve? What's wrong?"

She tightened her grip on Jim's hand, seeking his reassurance and the comfort of his touch.

"I'd like to say that the only problem is a burglar breaking into your house and stealing your television. However, what with the break-in at Keith's office, I suspect—" He saw Andi's eyes widen and heard her quick intake of breath. He also saw the look that darted across Jim's face as his hazel eyes darkened and his jaw clenched into a hard line. He did not like it. It confirmed his suspicions that Jim would not be easily controlled.

Before Steve could say anything else, Jim turned to Andi. His words carried the feel of absolute authority and were said in a clear, firm voice. "This is what I've been afraid of, what I tried to warn you about. Because of me you're in physical danger." He gently caressed her cheek with his fingertips, then twined his fingers in her short auburn curls. "This is no good, Andi. You have no idea of the ruthlessness of the people involved in this. Milo Buchanan is a very wealthy and powerful man who will stop at nothing to get what he wants. And what he wants is me—dead. I can't allow you to continue to put yourself in a position where something could happen to you because of me."

Steve tried to inject a note of calming rationale into the conversation and assume some kind of control. "Let's not make assumptions before we know what's really going on. I didn't go into your house or touch anything. As soon as I spotted the broken pane of glass in the back French door and saw things scattered around when I looked inside, I immediately turned around and went back to my car to wait for you. On the chance that this is nothing more than a common burglary, I didn't want to disturb any evidence since you'll need to call the police and report it. If, however..." There was no need to finish the sentence. They all knew what the implications were and what the probable truth would turn out to be.

They left the pub after determining that Jim would ride with Steve while Andi drove to her house as if she had just arrived home from vacation. Jim and Steve would park a couple of doors down the street and wait for Andi's signal.

The two men rode along in silence for a few minutes as they followed Andi in the van. It was Jim who finally broke the silence. His voice was not angry or argumentative, but there was no mistaking his concern and edginess. "I might as well tell you up front, I'm not at all comfortable with any of this. I trusted people five years ago, strangers who assured me they could protect me—keep me safe so that I could testify. Well, one of those strangers set me up and I've been running ever since. The only thing that's kept me going the last five years was the hope that one day all of this would end and I could see that Milo Buchanan got what he deserved. Now I've been put into a position where I'm once again being told to trust strangers."

Steve gave a quick sideways glance at Jim, then returned his attention to the road. "Oh? I was under the distinct impression that you no longer considered Andi a stranger and that she did not think of you as a story she was investigating or a book she was researching."

Jim did not respond to Steve's pointed comment, choosing instead to make one of his own. "I consider *you* to be a complete stranger." He did not give Steve an opportunity to reply as he continued to let him know exactly where he stood. "I want to know about this informant you've uncovered. Who is he and how did you find him?''

"One of my contacts was approached by a man who said he knew someone who had information to sell. I know that sounds a little vague, someone that we don't know knows someone else who has information, but it's how things begin, then we build from there.''

"So, you've neither seen nor talked with any of these people. How about your contact? Does he know either of these two people personally?''

"No. That's why I'm being cautious with this bit of information. It almost sounds like too much of a stroke of good luck—too easy.''

Jim's head snapped around and he stared at Steve. His strong words left no question about his intentions or feelings. "Andi said she was going to meet with this informant. I was dead set against it before I knew the circumstances. Now I absolutely forbid it. I won't have anyone's life put in jeopardy because of me.'' His voice softened. "Especially Andi's.''

"Look—I understand your anxiety and sympathize with your apparent feeling of helplessness in this matter, but you've got to trust that I know my job.''

"Right.'' The sarcasm crept into Jim's voice in spite of his efforts to keep it neutral—sarcasm surrounded by antagonism. "The ever-popular *trust me* once again rears its ugly head.''

Steve put any further comment on hold as he slowed the car and pulled over to the curb. They had arrived at Andi's house.

Jim and Steve sat in silence and watched as Andi got out of the van and entered the bungalow, her movements not quite as confident as they should be. The expression on her face told of her anxiety over what she feared she would find inside.

Andi unlocked the front door and entered her house. A sob caught in her throat as her gaze darted around her once-neat living room. She hugged her shoulders with trembling hands in an effort to ward off the sudden chill that spread through her body. Tears welled in her eyes, threatening to overflow the brims and trickle down her cheeks. A sick feeling churned in the pit of her stomach. She felt violated, almost as if she had personally been the recipient of the destructive assault.

Every cupboard and drawer had been pulled open and the contents scattered around the room. They had yanked the cushions from the couch and chairs, overturned lamps, uprooted plants from their containers. Her insides quaked as she made her way through the mess to her office. File drawers had been emptied and books snatched from bookcases. Next she checked the guest room. She found the same type of vandalism.

The sick churning in her stomach increased in intensity as she surveyed her bedroom, her own private sanctuary. Everything had been torn apart—the dresser drawers had been emptied out on the floor, clothes had been pulled out of the closet, the sheets and blankets had been stripped off the bed and the mattress left askew on the box springs. Her legs turned weak and refused to support her any longer. She pressed her back against the wall, closed her eyes and sank to the floor—her senses numb from shock and despair. She could not muster the energy to go to the front door and motion for Jim and Steve to come inside.

Jim could not contain the anxiety that forced its way out. He turned toward Steve, his voice fearful. "She's

been in there too long. Something's wrong.'' He
opened the car door.

"Wait—'' Before Steve could stop him, Jim leaped
out of the car and ran across the lawn toward the bungalow.

A feeling of dread settled in the pit of Jim's stomach
as he stepped up on the front porch. The door stood
wide open. He cautiously entered the house, then stood
still. His heart pounded a little harder as he took in the
disarray spread out in front of him. He listened for any
sound. At first he was not sure he heard it then it became more distinct—the muffled cries of someone
softly sobbing. He moved through the jumble toward
the back of the house, zeroing in on the direction of
the sound.

Andi looked more like a lost child than a bestselling
author. She sat on the bedroom floor with her back
against the wall, her legs pulled up against her body
and her arms wrapped around her knees. A pattern of
mottled sunlight filtered through the lace curtains at the
window and played across her face, picking up the wet
highlights of her tear-stained cheeks. Her eyes stared
straight ahead, apparently not focusing on anything in
particular.

"Andi?'' When she did not respond, he knelt down
next to her and took her in his arms. He looked around
at the mess. The room had been ransacked in the same
manner as the rest of the house. He rose to his feet,
bringing her up with him, and guided her across the
room. They sat together on the edge of the bed, his
arms wrapped around her and his hand holding her
head to his shoulder. Her body trembled in spite of the
warm temperature.

"Andi..." He did not know exactly what to say, how to comfort her. "I'm so sorry about this."

She spoke through little sobs, the tears still wetting her cheeks. "I know what Steve said at the pub, that someone had broken into my house, but I didn't expect to find this. I've never had anything like this ever happen before."

Jim clenched his jaw. This was his fault, all his fault. Here it was, five years later and now another woman's life was in danger because of him.

"Well, I think we can rule out common vandals and burglary." Steve's voice cut through the still air, immediately grabbing both Andi's and Jim's attention. "Your television, VCR and computer are still here." Steve again noted the closeness and intimacy between Jim and Andi. It would make things very difficult over the next few days.

"Come on, Andi. Snap out of it. We don't have time for this now." Steve's manner was not exactly harsh, but it showed control and made it clear that he was in charge and did not intend to indulge any unnecessary emotional reactions to what had happened. "We've got to get this mess cleaned up and figure out exactly what's missing."

STEVE PUT AWAY HIS equipment after doing an electronic sweep of Andi's house. "Everything checks out okay. The phones are clean and I didn't find any listening bugs anywhere else."

It had taken several hours to put things back in order so that Andi could do an inventory of what was missing. She placed the handwritten list on the dining table in front of Steve. "As near as I can figure it, this is what was taken."

He picked up the list and studied it. "No jewelry or personal items of value?"

"No, all that stuff is still here, including my photographic and dark-room equipment. It looks like the only things taken were my research files and interview tapes on the Buchanan Chemicals book." The uneasiness jittered through her stomach. She felt the reassuring touch of Jim's hand come down on her shoulder. She placed her hand on top of his.

Steve glanced at his watch. "Not only is it getting late here, but my body is still on New York time where it's three hours later. I've got to get some sleep." He pointedly stared at Andi and Jim, allowing a slight frown to wrinkle his brow as he again noted the intimacy between them. "In fact, we should *all* get some sleep. I just checked in with my people in New York and a contact in Chicago. That little publicity blurb seems to have stirred up a lot of activity. Several names from the past are suddenly popping up out of the woodwork. We've got a few very busy days ahead of us."

Andi caught the look of disapproval in Steve's eyes and knew exactly what he was really saying. It was going to be a bit of an awkward situation. She knew Steve had assumed that he would be staying in her guest room, as he always did when he was in the San Diego area. She did not know what his assumptions were about Jim's sleeping arrangements, but as far as she was concerned, Jim would be sleeping in her room. She was still unnerved about the break-in. She wanted the comfort of his touch and the reassurance of his closeness.

She addressed her comments to Steve. "I put fresh towels in the guest bathroom and I've just made up the bed in the guest room for you." She offered him one of her best smiles, trying to lighten the tension that filled the room. "I think I'm going to stay up for a little while. I'm too keyed-up to go to sleep right now." She saw the hesitation in Steve's eyes. She could almost see the thoughts running through his mind. She turned away from his stare.

Steve cleared his throat, showing an unusual nervousness that she did not normally associate with him. "Look, Andi—"

She did not give him an opportunity to finish his sentence. "Good night, Steve. I'll see you in the morning."

Steve hesitated for a moment, then apparently decided to let the subject drop for the time being. He went to the guest room, closing the door behind him.

Andi turned to Jim. She had noticed the way he had been following the conversation with keen interest. His voice was low and throaty, sending a little tingle through her body. His mouth curled in a teasing grin. "And just where do you want me to sleep?"

"Well...once again there seems to be only one room available." She returned his teasing grin, grateful for the brief moment of lighthearted banter. "I hope you don't mind sharing." She straightened up and assumed a look of mock seriousness. "I assume that we can both be adult about this."

He cupped her face in his hands and captured her mouth with a soft kiss. "I'm sorry about what happened to your house. It seems that no matter how much I didn't want you involved, others have conspired to take that decision away from me."

She rested her head against his shoulder and slipped her arms around his waist. The sob caught in her throat as she looked around the newly straightened room.

"Why did they have to do this? The files were clearly labeled and in plain sight in my office. Why did they have to ransack my house?" They stood together for several minutes, Andi drawing comfort from his strength.

It was Andi who finally broke away first. "It's a beautiful, clear night. I'd like to take a walk along the beach."

"I'd like that, too."

They went out to the patio and crossed the lawn to the stairs.

Steve pulled the bedroom curtain aside just enough to give him a clear view. He watched Andi and Jim walk across the yard to the back gate, then take the steps down to the beach.

As soon as they had disappeared from sight, he picked up the phone extension in the guest bedroom and dialed a number that immediately forwarded his call to another phone number. He made some notations on a notepad while waiting for someone to answer.

"This isn't going well, too many complications. We have to step up the schedule, speed things along. Hollander is real antsy. There's not a chance in hell that I'm going to be able to get him on a flight to Chicago, so it's going to have to go down here. That means we're going to have to revise the game plan."

"That's going to be tricky. Are you going to be able to get him to stay put for a few days until everything's ready?"

"I'm sure he's not going to take well to having nothing to do while being confined inside the house, but I'm going to have to work it out somehow. We don't seem to have any other choice." A hint of a cynical laugh traveled the phone line. "Starting with about five minutes ago when he and Andi walked out the back door and down to the beach.'' Steve changed the topic slightly. ''What's the word on Lou Quincy? How and where does he stand?''

''The U.S. Marshals Service has passed him over for promotion three times in the past five years and he's pretty bitter about it. He's coming up on retirement age and won't have as large a pension as he had anticipated.''

Steve paused for a moment to digest the information. ''Was it deserved or political?''

''It was a little bit of both.''

''What about that cousin of Lou Quincy's who was the court clerk for the judge who presided over the Buchanan case?'' Steve leafed through a small notebook but did not find what he was looking for. ''The mousy little guy who blended in with the woodwork but knew absolutely everything that was going on—where the bodies were buried, so to speak. What was his name?''

''You mean Theo Gunzleman?''

''Yes, that's him. What's his status?''

''That's a good question. He seems to have dropped out of sight. He quit his job four years ago, then a couple of weeks later left town. Whether or not Lou knows where he is, I couldn't say. I'll make contact with Lou and see if I can get any information on Theo.''

ANDI AND JIM WALKED ALONG the beach hand in hand. They found a large rock and sat down. He put his arm around her shoulder, but it was more of an absentminded gesture than a purposeful action. He had been doing his best to not let his disappointment show in either his words or actions. The tape had been stolen. His one and only possibility of a lead had gone up in smoke. And Steve Westerfall...Jim could not put his finger on exactly what bothered him, but an uneasy feeling persisted where Steve was concerned. Andi obviously trusted Steve Westerfall, but Jim did not share that feeling.

Andi snuggled her body against his. She listened to the gentle sounds of the waves as the soft breeze ruffled through her hair; she took in a deep breath, filling her lungs with the clean ocean air. "There's something so calming about the ocean. No matter how bad things seem, I can always come out here and feel better."

"Things will work out, Andi. They'll be okay." He gave her shoulder an extra squeeze, kissed her lightly on the forehead and projected a smile that said he had full confidence in the words he had just spoken. He wanted so much to calm her anxieties. If only he could calm his own. "Isn't that what you've been telling me for the past few days?"

She stood up and placed her hand against his chest, taking comfort from the rhythm of his strong heartbeat, and offered as confident a smile as she could muster. "It's very close, Jim. You heard what Steve said, things are moving very quickly. We're going to find the guy who made the second attempt on your life, find the agent who sold you out and link them to Milo Buchanan."

The smile faded from her face as she looked deeply into his eyes. "Then you'll be free—free to go where you want to go and free to do..." She could not finish the sentence. It meant he would be free to get on with his life, leaving her with a story, an ending for her book and a broken heart. She took a calming breath as she tugged at his hand. "Come on, we'd better get back to the house."

The tall man stood back, hidden behind the large outcropping of rocks. He watched Jim and Andi as they retraced their path along the beach toward the steps leading up to her yard. He continued to watch until they entered the house and were out of sight. He had been watching her house since early that afternoon. He had come by every afternoon and again in the evening, checking to see if she was back in town. She had finally returned, but was not alone. He made his way back to his car where he could continue to watch for a while.

MILO BUCHANAN HUNG UP the phone, then lit his cigar and blew out a long stream of smoke. He paused for a moment to savor its essence. "I'm not comfortable with this, Gordon. I never was overly confident in Ross Durant, but now that things are being stirred up I think our government agent is getting cold feet. I didn't like the nervousness in his voice just now, and I was especially unhappy with his attempt at a veiled threat. Ross Durant is looking more and more like a liability. It would certainly be tragic if some sort of *accident—*"

"Happened to him." Gordon finished his employer's sentence. "I'll take care of it, Mr. Buchanan."

"You do that, Gordon." Milo Buchanan leaned back in his large leather chair and took another deep puff on his cigar. "You do that."

Chapter Eight

Steve had been on the phone all morning, one call after another. Andi had been assimilating all the information that they already knew with the new information Steve had been gathering. It was a smooth working operation, one perfected over the years. Everyone was busy—everyone, that is, except Jim. He felt useless, restless and increasingly uncomfortable. He wandered over to the front window and stared out at the activity. It appeared to be a pretty busy place for a quiet side street in a residential neighborhood.

Jim's senses shot to full alert. He watched for a few more seconds, then turned toward Andi. "Someone seems to be moving in across the street and down one house. Were you aware of the house being sold?"

She joined him at the window and watched the two men carrying boxes from a motor home in the driveway into the house. "I guess it must have been rented while I was gone."

"Has the house been empty?" Something did not look right to him, but he could not put his finger on it. He continued to watch the two men carry the boxes inside the house.

"Yes..." Her voice trailed off as she watched what

was going on across the street. "I guess I didn't pay any attention when we arrived yesterday afternoon. There had been a For Rent sign in the yard for a couple of weeks before I left."

He turned his head toward Andi. "Before you left for Canada?"

"Yep. Before any of this started."

"Okay." Jim accepted the situation on the surface, but kept his eye on what was happening for a moment longer before turning away from the window. Was he letting his imagination run away with him? Something was still out of place. He felt it in his gut, an instinct he had learned to trust over the past five years. Would every car that drove down the street arouse his suspicions? He took a calming breath. It was just that he did not have anything to do. His thoughts returned to the picture of the two men carrying the boxes.

The realization dawned on him. The men were carrying stacked boxes. Unless all the boxes were filled with feather pillows, they just about had to be empty for the men to be handling them the way they were. And empty boxes meant they were not really moving in. And if they were not moving in, then what were they doing? The thought suddenly struck him that they were carrying only boxes. There had not been one piece of furniture moved into the house, not even a chair. He started to say something, but changed his mind. He did not want to voice his suspicions in front of Steve.

He turned toward Andi. "Why don't I go to the corner market and get some food? We skipped breakfast, but I'd be happy to fix lunch for everyone."

Steve immediately jerked his head up from his work.

"No. I don't want you wandering around outdoors in broad daylight where anyone could spot you."

Steve's unspoken words said that the more important reason was his need to know Jim Hollander's whereabouts every minute. He could not afford to have Jim slip out of his reach and disappear again...especially now that things were almost in place.

Andi's attention had been drawn to their conversation. "But wouldn't anyone watching my house have seen all of us yesterday afternoon when we arrived?"

"That was a careless slip on my part." Steve stared at Jim for a moment, remembering the way he had jumped out of the car and run across the lawn to Andi's house over his objections. "But that doesn't mean we can afford to go on making mistakes." Steve glanced at his watch. "Andi, why don't you order something for lunch, whatever you can get delivered—pizza, Chinese...I don't care what."

"Sure thing, Steve." Andi paused for a moment, a thought having just occurred to her. "We need to return the van to the airport car rental office here."

Steve pursed his lips and furrowed his brow in thought as he turned her words over in his mind. "No, I think we'll keep it for a couple of days. When I get this meeting with the informant finalized, we can use the van as a base of operation to house the recording equipment. I don't want to take a chance on wiring you. We'll insist that the meeting be out in the open so we can use a high-powered long-range directional microphone from the van and tune in on your conversation up to a block away."

"Hold it!" Jim refused to quietly stand by any longer. The tension was unmistakable and uncomfortable. Not only were others exercising control over what he did and where he went, he was being ignored as if he were not even in the room. "First of all, I resent being treated as if I had suddenly become invisible."

"And second?" The twinkle in Andi's eyes said she was teasing him with his own words, the very words he had uttered while they were in her cabin in the Canadian woods. "Whenever someone starts a sentence with the words *first of all,* that usually means there's at least a second point to follow."

Jim allowed a subtle grin to tug at the corners of his mouth. It had been an excellent tension-breaker. "Well, young lady, you seem to have a very logical thinking process."

She smiled at him, a fleeting show of relief touching her face, indicating that she was pleased he had accepted her attempt to lighten the mood.

Jim, however, did not allow the moment to linger. He turned his attention to Steve again. "Plans are being made that have a direct bearing on my life. I've said this before and I'll say it again. I don't want Andi meeting with anyone. It's far too dangerous. If there's a face-to-face meeting of some sort, it'll be with me or it won't happen."

He stared intently at Steve while turning a thought over in his mind. "In fact, with the interview tape gone along with the written transcription, there's no reason for me to be here at all." He saw the quick look dart through Steve's eyes, but did not know what to make of it or exactly how to read it. Irritation? Perhaps panic? Apparently his words had struck a nerve, just as he had intended.

"I understand where you're coming from, but it can't work that way." Steve took a calming breath and tried to keep the concern out of his voice caused by

Jim's implied threat to leave. "Do you have any idea how easy it would be for a hidden gunman to pick you off the second you stepped out in the open? And that's all they'd have to do, because the rest of us pose no direct threat to them. They'd simply blow you away and then disappear into the darkness of the night and it would all be over—everything would have been for naught."

Steve continued, presenting his case as clearly and logically as was necessary for the circumstances. "They're already aware of Andi. They don't know whether she actually knows where you are or not, but they do know that she's been doing heavy-duty research on you and the case. It would be logical that she would be the one wanting to meet with someone in order to further her research. Buchanan would not be so stupid as to harm the one person who might be able to lead him to you. I firmly believe that Andi will not be in any danger. If I thought otherwise, I wouldn't allow her to do it."

Jim awkwardly shifted his weight from one foot to the other as he digested Steve's words. "I suppose that makes sense." He shot a pointed glare in Steve's direction. "For now."

An awkward moment of tension was interrupted by the ringing of Steve's cellular phone. While he conducted his conversation, Andi used her phone to order some food.

Jim's restlessness grew with each passing minute. His nerves were on edge. As soon as Andi replaced the phone receiver in its cradle he let loose with the building anger that had been churning inside him. "I don't like being left out and treated as if things were none of my business. This may be some sort of a game, an adventure, nothing more than just a routine job as far as Steve's concerned, but for me it's literally life and death. You and Steve are busy, but I'm just standing around doing nothing—nothing, that is, other than being an obvious target."

She offered him a sincere smile, one that conveyed confidence and understanding. "The waiting is always the hardest part. I know what you're feeling."

He cocked his head and raised a questioning eyebrow in a skeptical manner. "Do you?"

"Yes!" Steve's voice carried the sound of excitement as he clenched his fist in the air. "We have the meeting. It'll be a two-step process. The first one will be tonight up in Los Angeles near the airport. If all goes well, we'll proceed with step two."

Andi's excitement matched Steve's. "Who am I meeting?"

"Joey is the go-between. We're meeting with him, then he'll introduce you to the contact whose name is Benny, no last name. Benny is the one who can finger the federal agent who is on Buchanan's payroll. Word is that this agent can name the person who attempted the hit on Jim and that he was actually present when Milo Buchanan personally ordered it. Benny also claims that this agent might be persuaded to talk to us personally."

Steve furrowed his brow in concentration for a moment. "That part makes me uneasy. If this guy has been in Buchanan's back pocket, then his sudden willingness to talk to us just might be a power play on his part to insure his own future."

"Why would that make you nervous? What difference does it make why he's willing to talk as long as he is?"

Steve addressed Jim's question. "If this guy is trying to pull off a power play by working both sides for his own personal profit, then he had better be very smart and very careful, because Buchanan just might be one step ahead of him. Milo Buchanan did not become as rich and powerful as he is by trusting to luck and assuming that everything is ticking along smoothly. If this guy has even hinted to Buchanan that he might be getting a little greedy, then he's probably signed his own death warrant."

"That might be, or—" Jim voiced out loud what had raced through his mind a moment earlier "—it might be a setup."

Steve made some hasty notes on his pad. "That's why we're taking it in two steps, checking out the informant first before proceeding any further. If Milo Buchanan thought we had a solid case against him, he could be out of the country in less than an hour. He's been stashing away millions in a numbered account in the Cayman Islands for the past two or three years, probably for just such an emergency."

Andi's gaze leapt toward Steve, his last words having grabbed her attention. She had not been aware that he had continued to gather information about Milo Buchanan's activities following the splash in the newspapers back when it had all happened. When she had mentioned the possibility of doing the book—it had probably been a year ago when the idea first occurred to her, then she set the idea aside for a while—Steve had told her that his research files on the Buchanan Chemicals case had not been updated beyond the furor following James Hollander's disappearance.

An attempt to mislead her? A deliberate lie? She dismissed the thought. It was probably information he had uncovered during the past few days. He had said that he had a new computer wiz working for him. That was probably the answer, that's how the money trail had been uncovered. In the back of her mind, however, was a nagging thought that there just might be more to it than that.

STEVE SLID OPEN the side door of the van, admitting the small man who had been hiding in the shadows of the doorway on the dark side street. Steve's voice was smooth and steady, setting a calm tone for the meeting. "It's nice to see you again, Joey."

Joey's dark, beady eyes quickly swept across the interior of the van, noting the other occupants. "Yeah…Steve. Sure…it's been a while." The quaver in his voice did as much to betray his nervousness as did the way he kept running his fingers through his thinning hair and clearing his throat.

Steve continued to set a calm tone to the meeting. "You remember Andi, don't you?"

"Yeah, sure…how ya doin', kid?"

"Just fine, Joey. And you?"

Joey did not answer her. He just kept staring at Jim, whose face was mostly hidden in the shadows. "I don't know this guy. What's he doin' here?"

Steve's practiced manner instilled a feeling of confidence as he gestured toward Jim. "He's okay, Joey. His name is Ron Pike and he's been working with me on this one." Steve quickly changed the subject in an effort to divert Joey's curiosity away from Jim and get on with the business at hand. "Tell me about Benny. How did you make contact with him?"

"Well…" Joey nervously glanced around the interior of the darkened van, then lit a cigarette as he stared out the front window at the empty street. "It's like I told ya, see. I was makin' the rounds of my usual Chicago haunts, droppin' a word here and a question there just like ya asked, when this guy comes up to me and tells me he heard I was lookin' for some information. He dropped the name of a guy I know, says that's where he heard that I was askin' around. He said he was hopping a flight to L.A. the next day. His name's Benny. He said he was beginnin' to feel crowded and wanted to get out of Chicago for a few days. I gotta say, Steve, I was sure surprised at your spottin' me a plane ticket. I ain't never been up in no plane before. So—" Joey cleared his throat, then emitted a nervous little chuckle "—here we all are in L.A."

Steve clamped his hand on Joey's shoulder and gave him a friendly smile. "Yes, Joey. Here we all are, in Los Angeles. So, let's go find out what Benny has to say for himself, shall we?"

The van moved slowly down the side street until it came to an area of warehouses and light manufacturing close to the Los Angeles airport. Steve turned off the headlights before turning into the alley adjacent to a warehouse. There was a small pickup truck parked half a block down the street. Steve put the transmission in Park but left the engine running. "Okay, this is it. Andi, you and Joey walk toward the pickup but don't get any closer than halfway. Make him come the rest of the way to you."

Joey nervously cleared his throat. "Yeah…sure. Uh…soon's I introduce the kid here to Benny then I'm gone—headed back to Chicago on the next flight."

"That's a very prudent idea, Joey."

Jim sat in silence, taking in everything that was happening. The knot in his stomach grew tighter and tighter as he watched Andi and Joey walk down the sidewalk. He did not like it, not one bit. It was not right, him just sitting idly by while Andi took all the risks in his place. It just was not right.

Steve brought out the recording equipment that had been hidden from Joey's sight. He adjusted the directional microphone and did a test recording of the casual conversation Andi had initiated with Joey so Steve could make sure everything worked properly.

Jim's worn nerves had reached full-tilt. It was all he could do to sit still. "Why are you letting Joey skip out, leaving Andi all alone with this stranger? Doesn't that put her in a very precarious position? Wouldn't she be safer with Joey there?"

"There's no way she would be able to count on Joey for any help if trouble popped up. He's done his part, now I want him out of the picture. Besides, an informant is usually more apt to talk if it's strictly one-on-one. No corroborating witnesses that way."

Steve and Jim watched as a man climbed out of the pickup truck and started up the sidewalk to the place where Joey and Andi stood waiting. Joey made the introduction, then beat a hasty retreat in the opposite direction and disappeared into the shadows.

Andi studied Benny for a moment. In contrast to Joey, he was a big man. The big was not really muscle, but it was not flab, either. It was more in the nature of just bulkiness. His eyes were in constant motion, his gaze shifting from place to place but never landing on her. He had a nervous twitch at the corner of his mouth. She had never seen him before nor had she ever heard of him. It was true that she had not been actively involved in investigative reporting for a number of years, but she still maintained some of her ties from the old days.

"Okay, Benny. Tell me what you have."

"Hey, like I told Joey...I know the guy you're lookin' for, the fed what's workin' for the man."

"*The man*...who are you talking about, Benny?" She needed to get him to name names, not put the words in his mouth.

He nervously shifted his weight from one foot to the other as he did another visual sweep up and down the street. Then he turned his eyes directly on her for the first time. His look was hard, not really menacing but a far cry from endearing. His voice became a harsh whisper. "Look, lady...we both know who I'm talkin' about here. I'm walkin' on dangerous turf and I ain't in no mood to play no stupid little games. Now, I can give you the name you want. I can finger the fed for you...for a price."

"A price?" She expertly widened her eyes in surprise, a practiced maneuver she had used many times in the past. "What kind of money are you talking about?"

"I ain't speakin' for no one but me. I want ten grand, cash only and in small used bills."

She forced a slight hint of panic into her voice in an attempt to further her cover story. "Benny...I'm just researching a mystery novel, not looking to be the next crime-busting superhero. Where would I get that kind of money?"

"That ain't my problem. Maybe your publisher would contribute since he's the one what's gonna be makin' the dough off it."

She looked at him quizzically, attempting to convey a little bit of confusion and uncertainty. "Suppose my publisher does advance me that much money, exactly what would it buy me?''

"That buys you an introduction to the federal cop. It's up to you to set your own deal directly with him. I hear he's developed a sort of nervous condition of late and is lookin' to take a little trip abroad in hopes it will improve his health.''

"I'll have to check with my publisher. Where can I reach you?''

Benny handed her a phone number scribbled on a piece of paper. "This is my pager. Leave your number and I'll get back to you. You only got twenty-four hours, after that I can't guarantee I can put you in touch with this guy.''

She took the paper from him and put it in her pocket. "Right...twenty-four hours.''

Andi started toward the van, then paused and turned back. "Oh, one more thing, Benny.'' She forced a casualness to her voice, as if what she was about to say was nothing more than an afterthought. "My primary interest in this isn't really Milo Buchanan or the federal agent or even the court case. I want to find James Hollander so I can interview him for my book. Does this agent know where Mr. Hollander is at this time?''

A crooked grin played across Benny's mouth. "I was sorta under the impression that *you* knew where Hollander was hiding.''

She studied him for a moment, trying to determine if he actually knew something or was just playing the game. "If I knew, I sure wouldn't be standing here talking to you. I'll be in touch in twenty-four hours.''

Andi watched as Benny returned to his pickup truck, then she hurried back to the van. Steve opened the door and she hopped in, sliding the door closed behind her.

Steve rewound the tape as he questioned Andi. "What's your take on Benny? Do you think he really knows anything? That's quite a hunk of change he wants just to put you in touch with this guy."

Andi thought for a moment. "The way he put it, it sounded as if the fed would be willing to personally implicate Milo Buchanan in exchange for a sack full of money and safe passage out of the country. I'm sure he finds that idea preferable to a jail term, which is what he would be looking at if he came clean with his department. Of course, the jail term would be better than what Buchanan would do to him. If all of this comes together the way it's beginning to look, we could have Buchanan on conspiracy to commit murder—a much more damaging charge than the ones originally brought against him five years ago."

"It's all too easy." It was the first thing Jim had said in quite a while. "Why would this government agent be willing to meet with Andi? Why would he put himself in jeopardy for the sake of some research on a novel, even with the lure of a big payoff? Is it possible that they know there's a lot more going on here than just a mystery writer looking for material? I find it all very questionable."

Andi looked from Steve to Jim, then back to Steve. "That's what I thought, too. Why would this guy be willing to come out in the open just to meet with a writer doing background research for a novel? He's got to know that there would never be the type of big bucks available from a book publisher that he could get from someone else for the information he has for sale."

IT WAS VERY LATE that night when they arrived back at Andi's house in La Jolla. As they had the night before, Andi and Jim closed the door to her bedroom and shut out the world. They lay quietly in bed, Andi snuggled in his embrace as he gently stroked her skin.

Even though Andi had become very important to Jim, he still wrestled with several thoughts, not the least of which was his very real concern over the direction things were headed. It seemed to him that he was being shoved farther and farther into the background, almost as if he were a nuisance rather than someone who had a major stake in what was happening.

He felt very uneasy about Steve's constant flow of incoming information and the fact that he refused to share very much of it. A persistent nagging in the back of his mind kept telling him he should not be passively standing by, accepting everything that was going on at face value. *Trust me…* he had been that route before and the results had been disastrous. The thoughts continued to circulate through his mind as he dropped off to sleep.

"DAMN! THAT BLOWS IT ALL to hell!" Steve hung up the phone, his angry words immediately grabbing Andi and Jim's attention. He surveyed the living room, as if looking for something. "Where's the morning newspaper?"

"What's the matter, Steve?" Andi handed him the paper she had just retrieved from the front porch.

"A little news item that may or may not make it into the San Diego newspapers. It seems that one Ross Durant, an employee of the federal government, was found dead in his car. The official statement said that he apparently fell asleep at the wheel and ran off the road." Steve quickly scanned the paper for any mention of the incident.

"You think he was the person Benny was referring to last night?" Andi looked over Steve's shoulder, glancing at the newspaper.

Jim added his thoughts. "I remember him. He was assigned to me while I was in protective custody after I got out of the hospital and was part of the transition into the witness program. He was certainly in a position to provide Buchanan with the information."

Steve put down the newspaper and turned toward Jim, a quizzical expression on his face. "Could he have been the one who made the second attempt on your life?"

"No, I don't think so. That voice was nothing like Ross's. The killer had a deep, raspy voice—almost like something out of an old gangster movie. I don't recall having ever heard the killer's voice before, but I'd sure know it if I heard it again."

Jim furrowed his brow in concentration for a moment. "This is sure a rotten bit of luck. If he could have named Buchanan directly, it would have given us—"

"There wasn't any luck involved in this, bad or otherwise. According to the source I was just talking to, the real story is that Durant was dead before the car ever went off the road. I would surmise that his greedy play for money alerted Milo Buchanan to his attempts to play both ends against the middle and caused the sudden *health problem* Benny mentioned. Buchanan simply decided to tidy up some loose ends."

"So, where does this leave us?" Jim asked his question before Andi had a chance to ask the same question. "It looks to me as if we're at a dead end." *And I should be packing my bag and getting the hell out of here right now.* But that was a thought he decided to keep to himself for the time being, at least until he knew all his options.

"Not at all. We can now comfortably surmise that Ross Durant was the leak. There's no reason for Benny to think that Andi would know who Durant was or what connection he had to the case. Even if he did suspect that her research might have turned up Durant's name, there's no reason for her to know about a routine traffic death that happened two thousand miles from here. There's nothing in your local newspaper about Durant's death. We'll go ahead and contact Benny just like we arranged."

Jim furrowed his brow in confusion. "How does this get us to Milo Buchanan? Benny had a contact with Ross Durant, but that doesn't put him anywhere near Buchanan. In fact, it would seem to me that in light of what happened to Durant that Benny would find himself a deep hole to hide in and pull it in on top of him."

"Exactly." The knowing grin tugged at the corners of Steve's mouth. "And he'll probably need to score some quick cash in order to do that. I've listened to the tape of last night's meeting several times and I think Benny probably knows the identity of the hit man."

Andi slipped her arm around Jim's waist and looked up at his worried face. "Steve knows his job. He has contacts all over the world." She allowed a teasing grin. "After all, he was able to discern that Jim Richards had only existed for the time he had worked at the resort, and he did that in a foreign country with less than two days to come up with the information."

The teasing grin faded from her face when she saw the seriousness in his eyes.

"Yes…so much has happened in the last few days that I had almost forgotten how all of this started." The sadness in his voice hung heavily in the air. He did not know what he was feeling at that moment. His entire existence had turned into an emotional roller coaster ride. Every time he thought the nightmare ride was about to come to an end, it would suddenly take another death-defying plunge into the unknown.

Chapter Nine

A slight scowl lingered on Steve's face as he watched Andi and Jim. "Andi...I'm going to be gone for a day or two. Call the car rental agency and see if they can pick up the van. I don't want you and Jim to take a chance on being spotted at the airport. In fact—" he turned his attention directly on Jim "—I don't want you to go outside at all."

Jim started to protest being given orders, but Andi spoke before he had a chance to say anything.

"You're leaving?" The surprise in her voice was unmistakable. This was the last thing she had expected from Steve. He had not talked to her about the decision or the reason behind it. This was not the type of working relationship they had enjoyed over the years. "Where are you going?"

Steve ignored her question. "I'll call you later today."

"But what about Benny? The deadline is tonight."

Steve pointedly stared at her, his words emphatic and precise. "I'll call you later today." He left no room for further conversation. He quickly packed his suitcase and left the house without offering an explanation or additional instructions.

Jim and Andi watched through the front window as Steve drove down the street. When Steve was out of sight, Jim turned to her. His last vestige of control over an uncertain situation finally deserted him. His voice contained an unmistakable frustration tinged with a growing irritation. The limits of *trust me* had just been exceeded.

"What the hell is going on here, Andi? Why did Steve take off and where is he going? What are you keeping from me?"

"I'm not keeping anything from you. I..." His gaze was so intense that it caused a slight tremor to dart through her body. "I don't know what Steve has in mind. He didn't tell me." Her words were soft and had a distracted quality about them. "We'll just have to wait here until he calls." She was as puzzled as Jim about what had happened. Steve's sudden actions made no sense to her at all.

Sarcasm clung to his words. "I don't think so, Andi. *We* don't have to do any such thing." He felt the anger building inside him. "I can't—I *won't* just sit around here waiting for Steve to decide to tell us what he's doing."

He had allowed all of this to go on far too long. He fought to separate reality from his fears and suspicions. "I've tried to be patient. I've tried to be understanding. But from the time of our arrival in La Jolla, the three of us have been together twenty-four hours a day. Now all of a sudden this man who is a complete stranger to me takes off without giving a reason or destination and leaves us here with only questions and no answers. Maybe *you* trust Steve and accept his actions on blind faith, but I sure don't."

She placed her hand on his arm and looked into the

trepidation that filled his eyes. "If you can't trust Steve, can you at least trust me? Please, Jim. Give it another day. Whatever Steve's doing is in your best interest. I promise you."

He saw the pleading in her eyes and heard the heartfelt sincerity in her voice. It touched a warm spot inside him. Had he allowed his deep feelings for Andi to cloud his better judgment? Was he being taken for a ride and played for a fool? Why would Steve Westerfall be concerned with Jim Hollander's best interests? It was a question that gnawed at his insides. Nothing was going according to plan, and none of it made any sense to him.

He took a calming breath and tried to force his doubts away. If his feelings for Andi were real, then he should trust her. He walked over to the living room window and stared out at the street. Maybe one more day, long enough to see what results her meeting with Benny later on that night would produce. Besides, being in an isolated area of Los Angeles and close to the airport would make it easier for him to slip away and get lost in the shadows. No one would know whether he had stayed in the city or had gotten on a plane, and with such a large and busy airport as Los Angeles International it could be a plane to anywhere in the world. At least that would work in his favor.

He continued to stare out the window. Everything outside seemed quiet—perhaps too quiet. He tried to shake away the ever-present skepticism and the disturbing feeling that things were not as they appeared to be.

ACROSS THE STREET and over one house a lone figure stood at the living room window staring at Andi's house. He raised the rifle to his shoulder and adjusted the telescopic sight until the image was sharp and clear, the crosshairs squarely in the middle of Jim's forehead. "He's such an easy target. One little squeeze of the trigger and he'd be history." He lowered the rifle, then leaned it against the wall. He continued to watch Andi's house.

STEVE MADE A SERIES of calls from his car, then placed a call to Phil Herman. "That's where things stand now, Phil. The final arrangements are being put into place at this moment. I should have confirmation within the next few hours. I don't expect anything serious to happen until tomorrow night. My original thought was to have Andi go ahead and meet with Benny tonight. It would have been interesting to know what kind of information he would have passed along in light of Ross Durant's untimely demise. Unfortunately things aren't coming together as quickly as I had hoped, so she's going to have to stall Benny for an additional twenty-four hours."

He listened for a moment, then responded. "No, I don't think that's going to be any problem. After watching them for the past couple of days, I'm firmly convinced that he won't get very far away from her. He doesn't like it, but he'll stay put—at least until they've heard from me. He is an unknown factor, though. He doesn't quite fit in with what I was expecting."

He paused a moment as he collected his thoughts. "I also hadn't anticipated that they would be sleeping together. I've known Andi a long time and I've never seen her be so impulsive about getting involved with someone. If it looks like he's going to cause us a problem, I'll just have to take *sterner* measures to deal with it."

Steve concluded his conversation with Phil Herman as he arrived at a motel in San Diego. He checked in and went directly to his room. He made another call.

"It's me. Any progress yet?" He listened intently, a frown wrinkling across his forehead. "Damn! That's no good. We've got to have it secured before tomorrow morning or we could blow the whole thing. You'd better get that computer cranked up into double-time."

He finished the call, issuing some final instructions, then leaned back in the chair and reached for the Havana cigar and his lighter. Everything was in the timing. An hour one way or the other could make a world of difference. But first, the money had to be found. He couldn't do anything until he had control of the money.

Phil Herman leaned back in the large leather chair. He carefully measured his words. "I was quite surprised to get your phone call, especially when you told me you wanted to discuss the Buchanan case. What prompted this after all these years? I didn't realize you were even seriously considering it as an open case."

"I appreciate your coming in to talk to me, Phil. As you know, Ross Durant was killed in an automobile accident." Frank Norton took the file folder from his desk drawer and dropped the newspaper clipping in it. "At least that's what has been reported by the press. It's not too surprising, really. He's been a loose cannon of late, trying to promote some sort of personal agenda."

"I remember Ross Durant, of course. But I'm afraid I'm not following you. I fail to see what the accidental death of a federal agent five years after the fact has to do with the Buchanan case. And why call me about it? I retired five years ago.''

Frank placed the file folder on the corner of his desk. ''I thought you might be able to provide me with a little insight. Perhaps share your suspicions about the people involved in the case—you know, things that were never verified as fact but you suspected. What about James Hollander? Have you had any word about his location?''

''His location? You're way ahead of me, Frank. I don't even know that he's still alive. Have you had word that he's out there somewhere?''

''No...I guess that's not exactly what I meant. I wanted to know if you had heard any word about him at all...one way or the other.''

''Buchanan's people missed him with the car bomb, then as soon as he got out of the hospital he disappeared. I think it's likely that they grabbed him.'' Phil paused for a moment as he eyed the younger man. ''Or do you know something I don't know? Why this sudden interest in what is essentially a dead case?''

''You're not aware of the book that's apparently in the works?''

''What book?''

Frank picked up the file folder again, withdrew a different clipping and handed it to Phil. ''This book. It seems to have stirred up quite a bit of activity among some old acquaintances.''

Phil read the publicity blurb, then handed it back to Frank. ''I fail to see anything here that would cause concern for anyone. Lots of novels have some truth to their origins, but that doesn't mean that the author has any firsthand knowledge of the original happenings. To tell you the truth, it sounds to me like kind of a dull premise for a mystery, especially coming from such a good writer as Wayne Gentry. Have you ever read any of his stuff? Real brainteasers. This kind of thing just doesn't sound like his style.''

"Nevertheless, the word is that Buchanan has been sending his people all over the place trying to do something, but we haven't figured out exactly what.''

"I'm still a little unclear about a couple of things, Frank. Why are you still following this case after all these years to the point of maintaining an up-to-date clipping file? And what do you *really* want from me?''

Frank regarded his predecessor for a long moment before speaking. "I know you officially retired, but I suspect you've kept in touch with some of your old contacts. I thought you might be able to give me a line on where James Hollander might be hiding.''

"James Hollander? Didn't we just go over this ground? Do you honestly believe that he's still alive?''

"Well…'' There was a bit of hesitation in Frank Norton's voice. "None of my people can positively confirm it in that no one has actually seen him. However, if he is alive he's probably on the move with all of this recent activity. He'll have to surface sometime, and we need to make sure we're there to greet him and see that he's protected before anyone else can get to him. That's my aim. So…do you have anything I can use?''

Phil leaned back in his chair, tented his fingers together and studied his former work associate. A slight smile tugged at the corners of his mouth as he turned the conversation over in his mind.

"I'll tell you, Frank. This is very strange, an odd coincidence of timing. Have you ever heard of a reporter named Steve Westerfall?''

"Westerfall? Sure. He's one of those investigative types, isn't he? Works out of New York and is syndicated in lots of newspapers with a penchant for big-time headline-grabbing busts. Likes to make the police look like Keystone Kops. An ego bigger than the city of Chicago. What about him?"

"I hear that he's been asking a lot of questions about James Hollander for over a week now. He even flew out to Los Angeles a few days ago. I've been told that he has a web of questionable associates and informants all over the country. I don't know what he's trying to specifically accomplish, but whatever it is it apparently requires his personal presence in California. That must make it pretty big."

Frank Norton's voice sounded his displeasure. "This is an open case and James Hollander is a government witness. If this hotshot reporter is doing anything to impede an investigation or has access to or is withholding any information vital to the case that should be turned over to me, then I'll see that charges are brought against him."

"Whoa! Back off a minute, Frank." Phil shifted his weight in the chair, an awkward movement that defined his sudden discomfort. "I only said that he's been asking questions and flew out to Los Angeles. That certainly doesn't mean that he can produce Hollander, or that he even knows where the man is hiding...or whether he's even alive."

"What's the matter, Phil? You seem a little distressed. Have you said more than you intended?"

JIM SAT JUST INSIDE the French doors, sipping a beer while he stared out over the backyard. He watched as the sun dropped lower in the sky, creating the long shadows of late afternoon. The golden light might have warmed the hearts of most people, but it left Jim feeling cold and strangely alone. Since Steve's mysterious and abrupt departure, the day had taken on an uncomfortable feel of foreboding. Jim had become more and more troubled about the situation with each passing minute.

His one hope for a clue to end it all, the one thing strong enough to draw him out of the safe haven he had created for himself, was the lure of Andi's interview tape. And now that lead had been snatched away. That, followed by the mysterious death of Ross Durant, was enough to tell him to cut and run as far and as fast as possible before it was too late. The only thing that had kept him from disappearing into the tangled maze of the Los Angeles underground were his very real feelings for Andi and the knowledge that because of him she had become a target.

"A penny for your thoughts." Andi slipped her arms around his neck from behind. She had been standing across the room for the past five minutes watching him as he stared blankly across the horizon. The despair that covered his face pulled at her heartstrings. She wanted so much to be able to calm his fears, but she had only questions of her own—no answers. She did not know where Steve had gone or why, and it disturbed her more than she wanted to let on. And even more disturbing was the fact that he had not called yet. It would be dark soon. She had to make contact with Benny, but she did not know what to tell him.

Jim's voice was hollow, devoid of all emotion. He continued to stare out at the ocean as he spoke. "A penny for my thoughts? It would be a bad investment on your part. I don't have any thoughts. I'm just marking time.''

Andi leaned forward, resting her cheek against his head as she gave him an affectionate little hug. Her voice was a mere whisper. ''I'm so sorry you're having to go through this. I thought it would all be so straightforward. You'd listen to the tape and then we'd know how to proceed from there. I knew things would not be easy, but I hadn't anticipated any of this. I wish there was something I could do to make it easier for you, but once it's over you'll see that it was worth all the hassle.''

''That's what I keep hearing. So sorry...wasn't supposed to happen this way...trust me.'' He could not contain the sigh of despair combined with a hint of apprehension. ''I don't know, Andi....''

''What is it, Jim? What's the matter?''

''I...'' He stood up and carried his empty glass to the kitchen, placing it on the counter. ''Let's go for a walk on the beach.''

''You know what Steve said about our being seen outdoors.''

''Yes, I'm well aware of what *Steve* said. *Steve*, however, is not here. In fact, we don't even know where *Steve* is or what he's doing. Besides, isn't it pretty foolish of us to believe that no one knows we're here? It doesn't take a genius to see that you're no longer out of town, that the house is being lived in.''

He took a calming breath in an attempt to force his anxiety back down to a manageable level. ''We certainly aren't protected here.'' He did not like the sound of the sarcasm that forced its way into his voice and words. ''They could take us any time they wanted to and there's not a damn thing we could do about it. In fact, I don't understand why they haven't tried. And unless you're hiding a gun somewhere, we don't even have anything to defend ourselves with other than some kitchen knives, a mop and a broom. So, there's really no reason why we can't go for a walk along the beach.''

''We haven't heard from Steve yet. He said he would call. I need to talk to him, to find out what to do about setting up a meeting with Benny for tonight.''

As much as he hated to admit it, she was right about talking to Steve. And then, as if on cue, the sound of the ringing phone intruded into the room. Andi raced to answer it.

''Hello.''

Steve clipped his words as he rushed through what he needed to say. ''Call Benny right now. Feel him out about Ross Durant without mentioning the name, see if he'll offer any insight into Durant being dead. Stall him about the money. Tell him you need another twenty-four hours to have the cash in hand and arrange for a meeting tomorrow night. Make it midnight at the same place as before by the Los Angeles airport. I'll call you tomorrow afternoon.''

''Steve...wait a minute. Don't hang up.''

His impatience clung to each word. ''Make it quick, Andi.''

''How am I supposed to stall Benny, especially in light of what happened to Durant? He's not going to want to sit around and take a chance on being the next victim of an *accident*.''

''You're the creative one. Think of something. I've got to go. I can't stay on this line any longer, I'm not sure it's secure.''

Steve replaced the phone receiver in the cradle. He

had been staring out the window of his motel room as he talked to Andi and he did not like what he saw. The same nondescript dark sedan drove slowly down the street for the third time, apparently circling the block. Were the feds watching him? He had been keeping an eye out and this was the first possibility he had noticed, but that did not mean it was not so. Was his carefully constructed web beginning to unravel before he was ready? There were too many things up in the air and he was running out of time.

Andi stared at the receiver for a second before replacing it in the cradle. She tried her best to appear calm. Jim was already impatient with the turn of events, and she did not want to do anything to further exacerbate the situation, even though she was uncertain about what was happening.

Jim was at her side instantly. "What did Steve have to say?"

"He…uh, he said to call Benny and set a meet for tomorrow night instead of tonight. I'm to stall him about the money, tell him it will take another twenty-four hours." She looked up at Jim, slowly shaking her head, as if turning several thoughts over in her mind before she continued. "Steve was rushed and concerned about staying on the line for too long. I could hear the stress in his voice. That's not like him."

Jim spit out angry words, his patience totally exhausted. "I'm putting a stop to this right here and now. I'm being set up for something…" A shudder moved quickly through his body as he thought of the possibilities. "And if Steve thinks I'm going to just sit here and wait for everything to crash in on top of me, he's crazy. I don't owe him anything and I have no reason to trust him. He's playing too fast and loose with my life. This is a two-way street. If he wants my further cooperation, then he needs to give me some answers about what's going on here."

His words were heartfelt and exacting as he tried to explain his position. "My reason for being here in the first place no longer exists. No tape, nothing for me to listen to, no reason to hang around making myself a target. Catch the bad guys? We already know who the bad guy is. It's Milo Buchanan. My staying here isn't going to change that or cast any new light on it. The government agent who sold me out? Ross Durant— recently deceased, thanks, I'm sure, to Milo Buchanan. All the loose ends neatly tied up and disposed of...all, that is, except for me. If I continue to hang around here, I'll never live long enough to see that Buchanan goes on trial for his deeds."

He took her hand in his, his outer manner softening somewhat. "And it's not just me, Andi. Someone ransacked your house because of me. I'm staying at your house and you've been personally involved—against my expressly stated wishes—in a meeting with an informant on my behalf. That puts you in the middle of my mess and that can't be altered. You're in danger, Andi. I want you out of here, too."

He carefully turned the thoughts over in his mind before giving them voice. "I'll never be able to forgive myself if something happens to you because of me." He placed a tender kiss in the palm of her hand, searched her eyes for some sort of truth. "Come away with me, at least until I'm confident that you'll be safe."

"I've got to stay and see this through. I can't let Steve down. I've given him my word. It's true that I don't know what Steve is doing, but I trust him and I

know he wouldn't betray that trust.'' She closed her
eyes for a second as she took a calming breath. She
gently touched his cheek. Her voice carried all the
emotional turmoil that churned inside her. ''Please
don't ask me to choose between my word and my desires.'' She choked back a sob. ''Please don't leave.
Just another twenty-four hours…''

Jim pulled her into his embrace and held her tightly
against his body. He made yet another uneasy decision.
The first questionable decision had been to leave Vancouver Island and go with her to hear the tape. And
this one was even more questionable in its validity.

A withering sigh of resignation escaped his throat.
''All right…a little longer.'' He touched his fingertip
to her lips as he tried to quell the uneasy feeling re-
sulting from his decision. ''But not much.''

They each savored the moment of togetherness, then
Andi pulled away. ''I have to make that phone call to
Benny.''

She dialed the number of his pager and punched in
her number. Less than five minutes later her phone
rang. She grabbed it before the second ring.

''Benny?''

''Yeah. So, you got the money?''

''I…uh…I don't exactly have it in my hands at the
moment, but I've made arrangements for it.''

Benny snapped out his anger. ''What the hell are you
tryin' to pull here? I told you twenty-four hours—no
more. I ain't got the time to hang around L.A. waiting
for you to figure somethin' out. I'm outta here right
now.''

''No! Wait a minute, Benny. I've got the money. I
just don't have it in my hands yet. It's my publisher…he gave me a hard time about it. He's on the

East Coast, three hours later than it is here. By the time I'd convinced him that he'd get his money's worth, the banks were closed. He's wiring the money to me to-morrow. I can meet with you tomorrow night, same place by the airport, but not until late—about mid-night."

Her offer was met with silence. She held her breath, waiting for Benny to say something...anything. He fi-nally broke the silence.

"Well...I guess one more day won't hurt. You sure you're gonna have the cash?"

"I'll have the cash...and you'll have the name of the federal agent, right? And where to find him?" Then she added a thought that had just popped into her mind. "And information about anyone else who was involved and paid off?" There was a moment of silence before he responded to her questions.

"I know you ain't researchin' no book."

A twinge of apprehension swept through her. "I don't know what you're talking—"

Benny's impatience cut straight through her attempt at a denial. "Don't try to hand me no line of bull. I know what I know. Fact is, I'm looking to take a little trip and could use some extra spendin' money, so for an additional—"

Andi's stern voice conveyed a toughness born of ex-perience. "We had a deal, Benny. Ten thousand for the identify of the federal agent and not a penny—"

"But for another ten grand I can supply you with another name...somebody else who took orders di-rectly from the man and passed them on, somebody who was in the know on what was going on and gave information to the man. You show up with the addi-tional cash—*and* James Hollander—and I can deliver that name, too. But I ain't dealin' with nobody but Hollander. If he ain't there you ain't gonna get that other name. Call it my insurance policy, if you want.''

"What makes you think I have any idea where James Hollander is hiding?''

"Oh, you know, all right. And if you don't, then you better hurry up and find out. No Hollander...no name.''

"But wait a minute. How am I—'' The line went dead before Andi could finish her question.

The look of shock that covered her face as she hung up the phone spoke volumes. She turned toward Jim, her eyes wide with surprise. She glanced back at the phone, then at Jim again.

A sense of urgency and concern surrounded his words. "You look like you've seen a ghost. What did Benny want?''

"He...'' She plopped down into a soft chair, the shock still running rampant through her consciousness. "He said there was someone else in addition to Ross Durant. I took it to mean that someone else who worked for the government and was connected with the original case had been bought off by Buchanan.''

Jim felt the blood drain from his face and his body turn momentarily numb. Had he heard her correctly? His words came out in a hushed whisper as if he were afraid to even say them out loud. "Someone else? Someone in addition to Ross Durant?''

"Yes. He also said he didn't believe the story about my research for my book. He told me that for another ten thousand dollars and a personal appearance by you that he'd give us the name of the other man. He said he would only deal with you directly, referred to it as his insurance policy to make sure we weren't setting him up.''

Jim could not force his mind to make any sense of what she was saying. He shook his head in an effort to clear out the bewilderment. "You mean someone high up that everyone thinks is legitimate but who's really in Buchanan's pocket? My God! Where does it end?"

"There's no telling how many people he's corrupted along the way and how many of them have a connection to you and to the case."

"So, I really can't trust anyone. We're confident that the agent who sold out my location was Ross Durant. But even if this Benny person confirms that, it won't mean anything, because Durant is dead. And now we find out there's someone else who was pulling Durant's strings five years ago and that someone is still around. Maybe two or three someones, not just one."

He looked at her as the feeling of utter helplessness swept through him. "Where do I even begin? This other person could be anywhere. And after him, who else? Someone working in the police department, the U.S. Attorneys office, the FBI, the U.S. Marshals office or maybe the federal court?"

He abruptly turned away from her. Should he add *investigative reporter* to that list? The shudder caught him off guard. Did he dare think in terms of the possibility of Andi's involvement? The last prospect cut through to the very core of his heart.

He paced up and down the room like a caged lion. His pent-up frustrations threatened to explode as the nervous energy churned inside him. It was the same feeling that hit him when he had agreed to enter the Witness Protection Program—that he was better off on his own. He should have listened to his gut instincts back then, and he should be listening to them now.

He abruptly stopped pacing and turned toward her. "It's time for me to get out of here."

Her body stiffened. Her voice bordered on panic. "But you can't leave. The end is so close...Steve said so."

The scowl quickly covered his face and a hint of bitterness crept into his words. "Yeah...*Steve* said so—the absent Steve."

Andi felt the cold fear welling inside her. She knew if he really wanted to leave, there was no way she could physically stop him. "Please, Jim...don't leave." She leaned her head against his chest as she circled her arms around his waist. "I...I don't want you to go." She felt his arms tighten around her. "I know what we said, what we both agreed to, that there wouldn't be any promises or commitment—no strings attached."

She raised her head and looked into his eyes. Her voice was hesitant. Her words came out as a mere whisper. "But I—"

His mouth came down hard against hers, infusing her with all the heat of his passion and tenderness of his unspoken love. The pain and despair dug into his gut. He was not sure what she had intended to say, but he did not want to hear it. He had never felt so unsettled about a decision. When he had made the choice to reveal Milo Buchanan's activities, he knew it was the right thing to do. When he had chosen to slip out of the custody of those who were supposed to be protecting him, he knew that decision had also been correct. He also knew the only expedient thing to do was get out of Andi's house, out of La Jolla and out of Steve Westerfall's reach. He feared for Andi's safety if he stayed and feared for her safety if he should leave. It seemed to be a no-win situation.

Chapter Ten

Benny nervously licked his lips and quickly shifted the phone receiver to his other ear. "I did like you said. I told her I'd only talk to Hollander, no one else. She tried to say she didn't know nothin' about where he was, but I could tell she was lyin' to me. I didn't need to change the meet because she told me she couldn't get the money for another twenty-four hours. So that's just what we wanted, right? That part's good, right? Ain't that right?"

"Calm down, Benny. You sound like you're starting to come unglued. You've done your part. You can come on back home if you'd like to."

"No..." He slowed down his response. "She...uh, she said they'd only show themselves to me 'cause they already know me. They wasn't gonna show themselves to no strangers. That was part of her deal." As much as Benny wanted to extricate himself from the entire plan, he did not want to leave without his money—not only the original ten thousand dollars, but the additional ten thousand he had demanded. He had to get his money before anyone found out that he had passed on information about the existence of another highly placed person on Milo Buchanan's payroll. He thought about Ross Durant and a little shiver of fear darted up his spine.

"That will be fine, Benny. Once you've drawn them out into the open so Hollander can be positively identified, you're free to leave."

"But I ain't never seen this Hollander guy before. How am I gonna know it's really him?"

"That's not for you to worry about, Benny. Your job is to get him to the meeting site."

"Uh…wouldn't it be easier if you just went to her house and made her talk? Grab Hollander if that's where they got him hid?"

"No, it wouldn't be easier. She lives in a quiet residential area, houses rather than apartments. That indicates a neighborhood where people have known one another for a while and are familiar with the natural rhythm of the street as far as normal comings and goings are concerned. It's not exactly a secluded location, and after the break-in at her house, her neighbors just might be a little edgy. They could be keeping an extra sharp eye on any strangers. It would be too easy for someone to spot a vehicle or make an identification. No, Benny…it's much better for them to meet us in a dark, isolated location without the possibility of any witnesses."

"Yeah, I can see that now."

"You've done a good job, Benny. I'm sure we can find a little bonus for all your hard work."

"Yeah…thanks, Mr. Buchanan." Benny heard the click of the receiver on the other end, then he hung up. He wiped his shirtsleeve across his sweaty brow as he peered out the window of the small motel room. The sound of the jumbo jet coming in for a landing caught his attention, causing him to look upward in search of the plane. Being so close to the airport had caused several interruptions to his sleep...not that he had been able to sleep all that well, anyway.

Again, his mind flashed back to what happened to Ross Durant when he had tried to push Milo Buchanan for more money. It was the reason he had chosen to grab additional money from the writer instead. He would be glad when he had his money in his hand and was on a plane out of there—and definitely not back to Chicago. His hand trembled slightly as he poured a shot of bourbon in a water glass and downed it in one gulp.

"PLANE TICKETS, GORDON. We need to go to Los Angeles tomorrow afternoon. But first we need to pay a little visit. Call our friend and tell him we'll meet at the usual place—" Milo Buchanan looked at his watch "—tell him two hours. I have a couple of calls to make first."

"Do you think that's wise, Mr. Buchanan? I mean, you going to Los Angeles? No need to put yourself in a bad spot. I can take care of this. I know I missed him last time, but I can promise he won't get away from me again."

"Yes, Gordon. You are responsible for his still being alive. But after all this time I want to be able to confirm for myself that it really is James Hollander. I don't want someone running in a look-alike on us in order to force us into acting foolishly. I want to see him, hear his voice and see the fear in his eyes when he realizes that it is finally the end for him. Hollander has cost me a lot of money and untold amounts of irritation. I want to personally make sure that there aren't any slip-ups this time."

"Yes, sir, Mr. Buchanan. How many tickets for Los Angeles?"

"I think there will be three of us, Gordon."

JIM STARED OUT THE kitchen window, peering into the nearly black night. He started to look away when a movement by the back fence caught his attention. He tried to pick out exactly what it was without alerting Andi, but whatever it was had disappeared. *If* he had really seen something. Perhaps his imagination had started generating assassins at every turn and corner. Then he saw it again. He was sure someone was out there. Someone was watching the back of the house.

He tried to change the atmosphere that surrounded them without attracting undue attention to his actions. "Why don't you fix us something to eat? I want to take a shower." Jim offered her a comforting smile, one intended to smooth over any worries and instill a feeling of confidence. He did not want her suspicious of his activities. His doubts presented themselves again, that nagging question of whether or not he could really trust her.

She returned the smile. "Sure thing. I'll see what I can whip up. Any requests?"

"No. Whatever you fix will be fine."

Jim quickly retreated to the bathroom. He turned on the shower but did not get undressed. He put his ear to the door. When he did not hear anything, he opened it a crack to peek out. Andi was in the kitchen. Jim quietly slipped out of the bathroom and into the darkened guest bedroom. He made his way to the window and peered around the edge of the drawn curtain.

There it was again, a darkened figure moving across the yard. It had not been his imagination after all. He had seen someone and that someone was very real. But who? One of Buchanan's people? One of the government agents? Then an even more jarring thought occurred to him. Could it be someone following instructions issued by Steve Westerfall, someone with an agenda that would account for Steve's purposeful departure and continued absence?

He opened the window, inching it up bit by bit as silently as possible. As soon as it was open wide enough, he eased himself outside and dropped to the ground. He remained silent and still as he listened for anything that sounded out of place. Then he heard it. Someone had bumped into one of the patio chairs. The tension churned in his stomach as his insides drew up into taut knots.

Jim edged his way along the side of the house until he reached the corner. He took a calming breath and held it for a moment before silently expelling it. He did not know what he would encounter around the corner. He had not thought to find something to use as a weapon. He looked around to see if there was anything handy. The only thing available was the coiled garden hose leaning against the wall. He unscrewed the heavy metal sprinkler head and held it in his right hand while putting his left arm through the center of the coil and lifting the hose.

He cautiously stuck his head around the corner of the house just enough to get a view of the patio. He spotted a tall man, but could not see his face. The intruder had positioned himself between the French doors and the kitchen window with his back to Jim. It was now or never. He stole silently across the patio, a bitter taste filling his mouth.

"What the—" The intruder turned around just as

Jim swung at him with the sprinkler head, causing the blow to glance off his shoulder rather than making a solid connection.

Jim dropped the coiled garden hose over the stranger's head and jammed it down past his shoulders, pinning his arms against his body. He shoved the intruder to the ground and placed a knee at his throat.

Jim's words came out in a breathless rush as the adrenaline pumped through his body. "Not a word from you until I say so."

"Jim? What's going on out here?" Andi stood just inside the French doors. Confusion touched with just a hint of anxiety colored her words and tone of voice.

"I'm not sure. Whoever this is, he's been watching us. I saw him at the back fence, then again as he crossed the yard toward the house."

"I'll turn on the light." Andi started to reach for the switch.

"No!" Jim's response was immediate and emphatic. "We don't know who else is out here. Open the door and I'll drag this guy inside so we can see who and what we have."

Andi did as she was told. Jim wrestled the struggling intruder into the house, and she shut the door behind them and pulled the drapes closed before turning to see what was going on.

"Nick!" The shock that covered her face also surrounded her words. "What's going on here?" Her gaze darted between Nick on the floor and Jim standing over him.

Her response startled Jim. He furrowed his brow into a frown as he took a couple of steps back. "You know this guy?"

"Yes. This is Nick, the ex-fiancé I told you about."

Nick's angry scowl lit first on Jim, then turned to Andi. "What the hell's going on here, Andi? Are you all right? Who is this guy?" With Jim having backed off, Nick managed to struggle out of the entanglement of the garden hose and scrambled to his feet.

Andi offered no apologies for the treatment Nick had received, preferring instead to unleash her own anger at him. "I've got a better question that begs to be answered. What are you doing lurking outside my house? Why are you spying on me?"

Nick's angry scowl quickly turned to a sheepish expression of uncertainty. "I...well, I wasn't spying on you. I just..."

"You just what? It's over between us, Nick. I told you that six months ago, yet you continued to smother me with your presence. It got so bad I couldn't concentrate on my work and finally had to leave town to get a break from your incessant telephoning. Now here you are again. What were you trying to do?"

As soon as Jim was satisfied about the intruder's identity, he interrupted Andi by jumping in with a couple of questions of his own, something far more vital than rehashing old problems. "How long have you been hanging around?" He shot a quick glance at Andi, then returned his attention to Nick, his concerns and questions of a far different nature than hers. "Have you noticed anyone else who might have been watching this house?"

Nick scowled at Jim before talking directly to Andi. "Who is this guy? Who put him in charge of the world?"

"It's a good question, Nick." Andi's manner changed from angry to cautious as she realized where Jim was headed with his questions. "Have you seen anyone else hanging around? Some stranger who might have been watching us? It's important.''

Nick's attitude softened as his gaze darted back and forth between Andi and Jim and finally settled on Andi. The hostility in his eyes turned to wariness. "I can't answer your question until you answer mine. Who is this guy and what's he doing here?''

Andi and Jim exchanged a quick look before she responded to Nick's concerns. "I'm working on a project with Steve. This man—" she indicated Jim "—is one of our contacts. We need to keep him out of sight until Steve's ready for him, and he thought a private house would be safer than a public hotel. That's all I can tell you.''

She noted the hesitation, then finally the acceptance in Nick's expression. She allowed an inward sigh of relief that they would not be pursuing the topic of Jim's identity.

Jim, however, was feeling no such sense of relief. He pressed for answers to his immediate concerns. "That brings me back to my questions. How long have you been hanging around out there, and have you seen anyone else watching the house?''

Nick stared at him for a moment as he rubbed his shoulder in the spot where Jim's glancing blow had caught him. "So, Andi's hiding you here. That's all that's going on?''

Jim leveled a steady gaze at him, attempting to make it as menacing as possible, without responding to Nick's question. He saw the discomfort come into Nick's eyes, then Nick awkwardly shifted his weight from one foot to the other. Nick finally broke eye contact with Jim and glanced toward Andi, then looked down at the floor.

His voice was quiet and the antagonism had disappeared. "I've been here on and off ever since you got home. I saw the other man..." he paused for a moment as he furrowed his brow in concentration, then looked up at Andi. "Was that Steve Westerfall? Average-looking guy, dark hair, in his late forties?"

"Yes, that was Steve." A hint of anticipation tingled inside her. Could it be that Nick had seen something that could help them? "Now, go on with what you were saying."

"Well, right after I got here I saw you pull up in the driveway and go inside. Then a few minutes later I saw this guy—" he indicated Jim "—run across the lawn and into the house. Then a couple of minutes later Steve follows him."

"Did you see anyone before that? Anyone who might have broken into Andi's house and ransacked it?"

Nick's expression appeared more and more perplexed with each passing minute and subsequent question. He turned toward Andi. "Someone broke into your house?"

"Yes. Did you see anyone who looked suspicious?"

"This guy—" he indicated Jim again while allowing a hint of a scowl to cross his face "—is the only suspicious person I've seen. But, in answer to your question, since you've been back I haven't seen anyone else who looked out of place while I was here."

Andi and Jim exchanged quick looks. He put forth a silent question by cocking his head and raising an eyebrow, and she nodded her agreement.

Jim exercised authority over the situation by opening the French door and indicating that Nick should leave.

"Next time you've got something to say, knock on the front door rather than sneaking up on the back door."

Nick started to leave, then turned back toward Andi. "Do the police have any leads on whoever broke into your house?"

"We didn't call the—" She quickly caught herself before admitting that they had not involved the police. There was no need to give Nick any more information than he already had. "No, there aren't any leads."

The frown wrinkled across Nick's brow as he narrowed his eyes while staring at her. "Are you sure everything's okay here, Andi? I think you're holding something back."

"I'm sure. Everything's just fine. All I ask is that you honor our need for secrecy about my houseguest. And Nick—" her manner softened and she offered him a sincere smile "—thanks for your concern. I appreciate it."

His features softened from the hard look that had been there just a moment earlier. He returned her smile. "Any time. You know if you ever need anything you can call me." Nick hurried out the back door and Andi closed it behind him.

She turned toward Jim, a bit of a weary smile turning the corners of her mouth. "Well, that was enough excitement for one evening. According to Nick, there hasn't been anyone hanging around. It looks like we're okay for the time being. No one knows we're here— or at least they don't know that you're here."

Andi may have been relieved by the information Nick had provided them, but Jim's confidence did not quite match hers. "Yeah, so it would seem." A wrinkle of deep concern furrowed across his forehead. His words were at first tentative. He was not sure where they would take him.

"Don't you think it's strange that no one seems to be watching this house? Why would that be? They broke in and knew you went to Canada. It's been almost a week since we left Vancouver Island. By now they certainly know you're no longer there. It's obvious that someone is living here, in fact more than one person. Nick saw all three of us arrive and so could anyone else." He stared intently at her. "So, why are we so safe here? And why hasn't anyone tried to get to us since we arrived?"

"I...I don't know. Maybe Steve made arrangements...." The question was in her voice, but the words were left hanging. Her expression said she did not have an answer to his concerns.

Did he dare risk staying awhile longer? Could everything be over by tomorrow night following the meeting with Benny? He could not stop the scowl that crossed his face. Or would everything be truly over, including his life? He shook off the doubts. No matter how much he wanted out of there, there were still two things holding him to the time and place. He had to follow through with this door that had been opened, regardless of where it led. If he did not exhaust all possibilities, then he would never know if he could have put an end to his exile. And then there was Andi...he simply could not bring himself to leave her to face whatever was going to happen by herself. In fact, he could not bring himself to leave her at all.

In spite of Nick's observation that the neighborhood seemed to be safe, Jim still felt very uneasy. But just as it had all begun, Andi having an integral bit of information on an interview tape, it now continued with

Andi having set up a meeting with an informant who had an even more vital piece of information—something that apparently would not be produced without his personal appearance. But in the meantime, he did not intend to sit idly by and twiddle his thumbs. He had already done too much of that. After he ran back to the bathroom to turn off the water, he took a pad of paper and pencil into the kitchen and sat at the table. He motioned for Andi to sit down next to him.

"Let's put together a list. I'll write down everyone I can think of connected with the case and we'll cross-reference those names with the people you came across in your research, which will tell us what they're doing now. Between the two of us, maybe we can come up with the identity of this mystery man, or at least narrow down the list of possibilities to something manageable."

She felt the same enthusiasm that she saw on his face and heard in his voice. A new bit of information that had at first startled her and filled him with trepidation had now turned into a glimmer of hope. There was finally something for them to sink their teeth into, something tangible to work with until it was time for the next step.

"They may have stolen the tapes, my diskettes and all the information I had in my house, but I still have the notes I took with me plus my memory. I'll get the notes while you make your list."

They each worked diligently, putting everything down on paper. Jim racked his brain for every name he could come up with, anyone he had dealt with during that time.

"That's it—a list of everyone I can think of who I came in contact with from the time I walked into the

U.S. Attorneys office until the second attempt on my life." Jim shoved the sheet of paper across the table toward Andi. "How many of these names do you recognize?"

Andi spread out the notes she had brought back with her from Vancouver Island. They worked late into the evening, matching every name she had with the names on his list. They eliminated the names they felt confident were involved in the initial investigation only and were not involved in the later focus on the prosecution when his location had been compromised. They eliminated the names of anyone who would not have held a position higher than Ross Durant. They also eliminated everyone who was not in a position to have access to vast amounts of information.

It was after ten o'clock by the time they had finished. Their efforts had produced a final list of half a dozen people working in four different areas involved with the case: five men and one woman.

Jim looked over the list. "Sally Hanover was the administrative assistant in the U.S. Marshals office with access to the witness files, a real wiz with the computer who had both beauty and brains. Lou Quincy was in charge of the U.S. Marshals office in Chicago and approaching retirement age. He struck me as being bitter over his lack of career advancements. Cliff Turner headed the FBI's investigation and seemed to have a lot of expensive toys that should have been beyond the means of an FBI salary. Phil Herman was the U.S. Attorney who very quickly dismissed all charges against Buchanan, then immediately took himself out of the spotlight by resigning and taking an early retirement. Frank Norton was the Assistant U.S. Attorney who couldn't get his feet into Phil Herman's shoes fast enough, a very aggressive and overly ambitious man as I recall. And Theo Gunzleman was the court clerk working with the presiding judge on the case, a mousy little guy who sort of blended into the woodwork but had access to a lot of important information.''

He reached over and took Andi's hand and gave it a little squeeze. "This is the first thing I feel like I've accomplished since we left Vancouver Island. We should have done this as soon as we discovered your research material had been stolen.'' He leaned back in the chair and stretched his arms above his head.

"You're right. We should have done this a couple of days ago.'' Andi stifled a yawn.

"Tired?'' He reached out and gently caressed her cheek.

"Yes. It's been a long day. I think I'm going to turn in.''

"Me, too.'' He rose from his chair and stretched the kinks out of his back.

She checked the doors to make sure they were locked, then started to turn out the lights.

"Leave them on.'' A sudden urgency surrounded his words and carried over into his voice, as if a thought had just occurred to him. "In fact, turn on all the outside lights. As long as it's obvious that you're home, we might as well offer as much discouragement as possible to anyone who might be considering breaking in. With the outside lit up and the inside lights turned on, they couldn't be sure if we were sleeping or awake, and couldn't get close to the house without taking a chance on being seen.'' His gaze nervously darted around from door to window. "It's not much in the way of protection, but it's better than nothing.''

"Good idea." Andi immediately flipped on the switches for all the outside lights.

They had been so involved in their efforts for the past few hours with his mind so totally occupied, that he had allowed his feelings of trepidation and anxiety to be shoved aside for the time being. But now they erupted again, bringing back everything that had been of serious concern to him earlier.

He looked at her curiously, as if trying to make up his mind about something. He finally shared his thoughts. "If we go out the back door and down the steps to the beach, would we be able to walk along the sand to a motel were we could spend the night? Could we get away from here without anyone knowing?"

She slowly turned toward him. His words had brought out into the open the same concerns that had been running through her mind. So many things he said had also gone through her mind, things she slowly digested and tried to make sense of. She had not been happy with her lack of positive conclusions. Where was Steve Westerfall? Why had he suddenly left them there without any protection? And why had no one made any attempt to get at them? They were sitting ducks, just as Jim had said.

Maybe following Steve's instructions without question was not such a good idea. It created a moment of sadness inside her. She had always trusted him implicitly, and now she had doubts. Had he changed in the years since they had worked together, or had she never known the real Steve Westerfall? She looked at Jim, at the troubled expression on his face and the anxiety in his eyes. She had gotten him into this mess and it was up to her to try and get him out.

"Yes. There's a little motel about half a mile down

the beach. We can reach it without being seen from the road.''

He turned out the lights that illuminated the back of the house and the patio. ''Do you have a timer for these lights?''

She looked at him questioningly. ''Yes...why do you ask?''

''We need them off to get out without being seen, but I want them on all night as a deterrent to anyone who might want to get close to the house.'' He headed for the bedroom. ''You set the timer to turn on the lights in ten minutes while I throw a few of our over-night things in a pack to take with us.''

The decision had been made. They performed the necessary tasks, then they slipped out the back door and ran across the yard to the steps leading down to the beach. They quickly made their way down the beach, walking as fast as they could in the soft sand, ever mindful of the fact that the tide was coming in and shoving them closer and closer to the bluff wall. They finally arrived at the motel and checked in without incident.

Andi sank into the softness of the bed, took a calm-ing breath and closed her eyes. ''We made it. Now we can relax and get a good night's sleep. Tomorrow is going to be a very long day, especially with the late-night meeting in Los Angeles with Benny.''

Jim whirled around to face her. Had he heard her correctly? ''You aren't still planning to go through with that, are you? The whole thing reeks of a setup.''

''We have to, Jim. How else are we going to find out which one of those names on our list is the culprit, assuming it is one of those names? Whoever it is has hidden his—or her—activities very well and has done a superb job of covering any tracks.''

Jim sat down next to her. ''I don't know.'' He held her gaze for a moment as if turning something over in his mind, then leaned his face into hers and placed a loving kiss on her lips. ''Maybe...since Benny's criteria seems to be my presence rather than yours...''

''We'll *both* be there.'' She wrapped her arms around his waist as he drew her into his embrace. Any further concerns about the meeting were lost as physical desire combined with the closeness of an as yet unspoken love.

Chapter Eleven

Steve Westerfall parked his car at the curb across the street from Andi's house, then checked the time—almost midnight. He stared at her bungalow with all the lights on, both inside and out. Something was wrong…very wrong. He dialed her phone number again, the third time in the last half hour. And just as with the previous two times, it was her answering machine that picked up the call.

He sat for a moment, staring at the house. Andi had his pager number but had not used it. He did not know whether to be angry that they had left the house against his express orders, especially without bothering to notify him, or worried about what the reason might be for them being unable to answer the phone. Either way, he had somehow lost control of the single most important element of his plan…the fact that he had James Hollander on ice until he needed him—or at least he had thought so.

Steve's thoughts were interrupted by his cellular phone. He grabbed it on the first ring, his voice angry. "Where are you?"

"Steve?" The feminine voice did not belong to

Andi. "What do you mean by that? I'm at home shackled to my computer and I think I've found it."

"Found it?" It took a moment before Steve got his head and thoughts turned around. He had been so sure the call would be from Andi. Suddenly everything clicked in his head. His excitement charged through the phone. "The money? You've cracked the numbered accounts?"

"Yep. I kept digging into Buchanan's money trail. He's done a good job of obscuring it and hiding things, but I finally locked in to the key. I have two accounts and six million dollars so far."

"Only six million? I was sure there was a lot more than that."

"I'm sure there's one more account. I've almost got it, but I need to do a little more digging."

Steve could not stop the broad smile that spread across his face. "Sweetheart, if you were here right now I'd kiss you like you've never been kissed before."

A low, throaty laugh greeted his outburst, followed by clearly teasing words. "Promises, promises. Actions speak louder than words and you seem to be all talk."

Steve's words turned serious. "Have you tapped into the airline records and found Buchanan's plane reservations yet?"

"Yes, all *three* of them."

"So, they're together. That's pretty foolish. Buchanan must be more eager than I thought. Everything is coming together perfectly." Steve glanced at Andi's house with all the lights glowing brightly. Well, *almost* everything. "Can you do the funds transfer without any problem?"

"Yes. You want it done as soon as his flight takes off and they're in the air?"

"Yes. As soon as Buchanan is in a position to no longer be able to easily deal with any business situation."

"What about the third account? If I haven't found it by the time we need to do the transfer of the funds, do you want me to continue looking for it?"

"I sure do. You keep looking and transfer that money the moment you find it."

Steve disconnected from the call and returned his attention to his current problem. He continued to stare at Andi's house. Why wasn't she answering the phone? He wanted to go up to the house and check, but did not dare with all the outside lights on. A bit of an appreciative grin tugged at the corners of his mouth. He did not know whose idea it was to light up the outside of the house and the yard, but he suspected it had been Jim Hollander's idea and it had been a good one.

He dialed another number. "She's not answering the phone. What's going on?"

"As far as I know, nothing's going on. There's been no activity since they turned on all those lights."

"Nothing? Are you sure?" Steve's irritation at the lack of information bristled over the phone.

"Well…a few minutes after they turned on all the lights the backyard lights went out for about ten minutes, then came back on and have been on ever since. The man from down the street walked his dog just like he does every night. The couple two doors up had a pizza delivered. Other than that the block has been quiet."

"Okay. I'll check with you later." Steve disconnected from the call and thought about the information he had just received. The ten-minute span when the backyard lights had been off must have been when Andi and Jim slipped out. They could have gone either direction along the beach without being spotted. He finally came to the conclusion that the plan had been a result of Jim Hollander's uncanny survival instincts. But the questions remained...where did they go and would they be back?

JIM SAT ON THE EDGE of the bed while he waited for Andi to finish dressing. He leaned back on his elbows as he looked around. Even though the motel room was small and sparse, it was clean and had provided them a safe haven for the night. But now it was morning again and it would soon be daylight. Decisions needed to be made. He had given it a lot of thought. There would be no more incidents of other people making plans about his life while leaving him in the dark. He desperately needed to regain control.

"Well, I'm ready." Andi replaced the last of her toiletries in the pack along with Jim's belongings. She sat down on the edge of the bed next to him. "So...what now?"

He took her hand in his. "I've been giving it some thought. My first instinct was to keep on going. But now that I've gone over everything in my mind, I think we should go back to your house. I want you to put in a call to Steve's pager and—"

"Steve... I wonder if he tried to get in touch with us last night to find out the results of my conversation with Benny. If he did, then he's probably furious about our taking off without letting him know."

A scowl crossed Jim's forehead as he clenched his

jaw in a tight line. "You can tell Steve it's a two-way street. If he expects people to keep him apprised of their whereabouts, then he needs to make sure those same people are made aware of his plans."

He unclenched his jaw. "As I was saying, put in a call to Steve and tell him I demand a face-to-face meeting with him right away, that I'm not showing my face in some dark alley tonight until he and I iron out a few problems and he satisfies me about what's going on. That should produce some results."

Andi eyed him curiously. "Do you think that's wise?"

"I think it's a reasonable request, considering..."

He did not need to say any more. Andi understood exactly what he meant and where his anxiety came from. She, too, had been giving the situation a lot of thought. She felt as if she were being pulled in two directions. Her loyalty and trust where Steve Westerfall was concerned had always gone without saying. But now she had to agree with Jim that Steve's actions were very curious—she could even call them suspicious without fear of contradiction.

"Do you want me to call him now and have him call back here?"

"No, let's do it when we get back to your house. There's no need to let anyone know we used this motel. We might need to do this again." The words had slipped out without him realizing their impact until it was too late. He had just committed to staying at least one more night.

Jim picked up the pack, put his arms through the straps, then took her hand in his. "Let's go."

They walked back along the beach as the first gray streaks of dawn began to penetrate the night sky. Andi started up the steps to her backyard, but Jim stopped her before she reached the top.

"Wait a minute. Let's check it out first." He edged past her until he could see over the rim of the bluff. The outside lights continued to illuminate the house and surrounding area. He scanned the yard and the neighbors' houses. One house was dark and the other had lights on in a couple of rooms that appeared to be a bathroom and a bedroom. Everything looked okay. If someone had been planning to make an attempt on the house, they would have done it before the neighbors woke up.

He turned to face Andi. "It looks all right. Let's make it quick, though. I'll go first."

"I'm right behind you."

They dashed across the lawn and into the house. Jim did a quick survey of the interior. "Nothing seems to have been disturbed." He pulled aside the edge of the drape at the living room window just enough to see outside. "Nothing untoward out here, either. So, how about some..." A warm smile lit up his face.

"I'm ahead of you." Andi measured the coffee into the filter, then poured the water into the coffeemaker.

As soon as the coffee was ready, she poured a cup for Jim and for herself. Next she placed a call to Steve's pager. Jim gave her some quick instructions on what to say when Steve returned the call. "When the phone rings just act natural, as if we've been here all along. Give him the results of your conversation with Benny, then turn the conversation over to me and I'll give him my demands."

"What if he tried to get in touch with us last night and knows we weren't here?"

"Let him be the one who tells you that, don't volunteer the information. Then let me talk to him."

Their conversation was interrupted by the ringing of the phone. She grabbed the receiver from the cradle.

Steve's angry voice did not wait for her to say anything. "Where the hell have the two of you been? I tried to call several times and all I got for my trouble was your answering machine."

Steve's verbal attack surprised her. He was normally a very controlled person. However, nothing was any longer *normal.* Things were very tense, with everyone's nerves exposed and on edge. Andi was no exception. "Where the hell have we been? I've got a better question. Where the hell have you been and what have you been doing? You walked out and left Jim and me sitting here without a clue as to what was happening or what was going on inside your head. We could have been dead for all you knew. I can't begin to tell you how—"

Jim took the phone from her. Now was not the time for unleashing anger. He briskly clipped his words, showing neither warmth nor anger. "Steve, we need to talk and we need to do it now."

"Fine, what's on your mind?"

"Not on the phone. I want a face-to-face meeting with you right now. You get no further cooperation out of me until you tell me exactly what's going on and what you have planned. There's no way I'm showing up in some dark alley until we've gotten a few things straightened out." There was a pause. Jim waited for Steve to respond to what he had said.

"I take that to mean Andi was successful in putting Benny off until tonight." It was a piece of information

Steve already knew, but he was not ready to share that knowledge.

"Maybe it does and maybe it doesn't. When do we talk?"

"Okay. I can be there by lunch. Now, let me talk to Andi again."

Jim handed the phone back to her, then leaned against the kitchen counter sipping his coffee.

Andi had calmed down a little from her outburst, but not much. She snapped out the words. "What do you want?"

"This is no time for petulant behavior, Andi. Now, let's get on with the business at hand. Tell me what Benny said."

She could not totally erase the sharp edge from her voice. "I thought you already knew since you never bothered to check back to find out if there was a meeting still set for last night." It was a thought that had been swirling around inside her head, but one she had not given serious consideration to until the words were out of her mouth. Just exactly how much did Steve already know and how did he know it? And why was he keeping it from them?

"I told you it had to be changed and I trusted that you were able to accomplish it. Now, what specifically did Benny say?"

Andi was not satisfied with his answer. For the first time since she had known Steve, she felt as if she did not know him at all. She recalled his looking at the piece of paper Benny had given her with his pager number on it. Had Steve been in contact with Benny on his own? Again, she returned to the same thought— why the deception?

"He didn't say anything about Ross Durant's death.

He did say there was someone else besides Durant who was also on Buchanan's payroll and for an additional ten thousand he'd give me that name, too. In addition to the money he insisted that Jim be present. When I tried to tell him that I didn't know where Jim Hollander was, he laughed it off and said he knew better—no Hollander, no name. The meeting is at the same place and same time as the last one.''

"So, he wants another ten thousand. Did you agree to it?"

Andi furrowed her brow and pursed her lips for a moment. Steve had shown no reaction to Benny's insistence that Jim be at the meeting or the surprise disclosure of another person above Ross Durant. Yet another puzzling bit of behavior coming to light. "I didn't really need to agree to anything. Benny apparently assumed that he would get what he wanted."

"Okay. I'll see you in a little while. I seem to have a command appearance for Jim's benefit." Steve's last words carried a touch of sarcasm. He disconnected from the call without saying goodbye.

Andi looked at Jim. "What do you think?"

"Judging by your end of the conversation, I'd say Steve already knew everything that was going on. He has some source of outside information that's keeping him apprised of everything...except for what you and I know, such as when and how we left here and where we were last night." A hint of a bittersweet chuckle escaped his throat. "It's nice to know that there's one little thing where we still have some control."

Without saying anything else, Jim went to the bedroom and began packing the belongings he had brought with him. Andi followed him and watched for a couple of minutes.

"Jim?" Her voice was hesitant. "What are you doing?"

He did not turn around to look at her. "I thought it was obvious. I'm packing. After tonight…assuming that I'm still alive…I could well be on the run again. In fact, if my conversation with Steve isn't satisfactory, I could be out of here even sooner."

He took a calming breath, then turned around to face Andi. The expression on her face tugged at his heartstrings. More than anything he wanted to be able to lead a normal existence and have Andi be an important part of his life. He allowed a little sigh of resignation. But apparently it was not going to be. He reached out and pulled her into his arms.

"I know I keep contradicting myself every time I open my mouth—I'm leaving…I'm staying…I'll wait and see what happens…I'm going to go along with what happens…I'm not going to cooperate—but things are rapidly moving from unsettled to rotten. Before this began I at least had control of my own decisions. Even that seems to have been taken away from me. Right or wrong, I need to regain control of my life…such as it is."

"I don't understand what's been happening here, either. I thought I did, but now I realize that I'm as totally out of the loop as you are." She looked up into the sadness in his eyes. "Yesterday you asked me to go away with you. Is that offer still open?"

The ringing of the phone interrupted the moment. Andi went to answer it and returned a minute later. "It was nothing, just a wrong number." She furrowed her brow in concentration for a moment. "At least I *think* it was a wrong number." She looked at him quizzically. "Do you suppose it could have been someone wanting to know if we were here?"

He shook his head in dismay and did not answer her question—this one or the one about going with him. "I need to finish packing…just in case."

Andi did not know what to say. For the first time she felt as if she had a true inkling of what Jim had been through for the past five years…not knowing who he can trust or what was real and what was a lie. It saddened her that she had begun to doubt Steve. Was this how Jim felt about her? Did he have doubts whether or not he could really trust her?

She took a steadying breath in an attempt to calm her nerves. "What time is Steve supposed to be here?"

"He said he'd be here by lunch. So, either he's busy with something or he's not in this area. Perhaps he's in Los Angeles…maybe meeting with someone?"

Andi shook her head as she stared at the floor, her voice soft. "I don't know, Jim. I just don't know…not anymore."

He pulled her into his embrace and rested his cheek against the top of her head. "Just a few hours and that will tell everything. Either Steve has some satisfactory answers or he doesn't. If not, then I'm out of here. My continued presence can only be an added danger for you." He continued to hold her a moment longer, but his thoughts were elsewhere as a plan began to take shape.

He glanced at his watch. It was only seven-thirty, which was nine-thirty in the morning Chicago time. "Andi—" his voice was hesitant as if he were thinking out loud "—we need to make some phone calls. Let's contact everyone on that list. You call half the names and I'll call half the names. That way, anyone comparing notes with someone else on that list might be thrown further off guard by not knowing if they were ultimately dealing with a man or a woman. We'll tell them we have some information to sell, that we know where James Hollander is hiding. Then we'll follow it up by saying we have it on good authority that he's leaving the country in two days, headed for Mexico. We'll say we've seen him and talked to him, but he's had plastic surgery and no one else knows what his new face looks like. Let's see what kind of reactions we can get with that.''

"Do you think that's wise?"

"Wise? As opposed to what? Sitting here and doing nothing? There has to be someone on that list who has some current connection with what's going on. Besides, it's Milo Buchanan who is the ultimate catch. His ego will force him to insist that he could recognize me, no matter what I'd done to my appearance.''

They both warmed to the task. The first order of business was to obtain telephone numbers. "It would sure be nice if you had a cellular phone in addition to your regular phone number. That way we could both make calls at the same time."

"Of course!" A triumphant smile spread across Andi's face. "Why didn't I think of it before? We do have another phone number. I have a separate phone number for my computer and fax machine. We can plug a regular phone into that so we can both make phone calls at the same time." She quickly unplugged the phone from her bedroom and took it to her office. She disconnected the phone line from her fax machine and plugged in the other phone.

With two separate phone lines now at their disposal, they set about procuring the phone numbers they needed. Half an hour later they began making calls. They knew it was a long shot. Neither of them truly expected much in the way of results from the exercise. They were primarily looking for any unusual reactions to their calls, someone who might be caught off guard by the call and would let something slip. It was also a way of keeping busy while waiting for Steve to arrive. At least that was the way Jim thought of it. He could not deal with any more inactivity, with the nerve-racking reality of waiting for something to happen.

Andi placed her call first. "Cliff Turner?"

"Yes. Who is this?"

"Never mind what my name is. I have some information that I think might be of interest to you. It concerns James Hollander. I know where he is."

There was a long pause on the other end before Cliff responded. "And why would I be interested in this James Hollander?"

A little tingle of excitement began to flicker inside her. Something about the hesitation combined with the tone in his voice told her that she had struck a nerve. "I'll tell you what. Why don't you think about this? He's planning to leave the country in a couple of days. He's had plastic surgery and I know what his new face looks like. You decide what that's worth to you and I'll call you later."

"Wait!" A sense of urgency surrounded his words. "Who are—"

Andi hung up before he could finish the sentence. She dialed the next number on her list. "Frank Norton? I have some information that I think might be of interest to you. It concerns James Hollander."

His voice showed immediate attention. "Hollander? Do you know where he is?"

Andi quickly straightened to attention. This was even more promising than her conversation with Cliff Turner. Frank Norton had not even bothered to ask who she was or pretend to not recognize Jim's name. "Yes, I do. I also know that he plans to leave the country in a couple of days and has had plastic surgery. I can provide a picture of his new face. Why don't you think about what that would be worth and I'll get back to you." She hung up before he could say anything.

Jim attempted to make some phone calls. His first call was to Phil Herman. All he could ascertain was that Phil had gone to New York the day before and would not be back for a week. On his second attempt he found out that no one knew where Theo Gunzleman was, that he did not work as a court clerk any longer.

He finally connected on his third call. "Lou Quincy? I have some information I believe will be of interest to you. It concerns James Hollander."

"I don't know who you are or what you think you're trying to pull, but let me set you straight. There isn't anything you can tell me. Hollander is a dead man and that's the end of that."

"No way, my friend. He's far from dead. He does have a new face, though. And he plans on leaving the country in a couple of days. Now, if that's of any interest to you, we can discuss what it's worth when I call back." Jim quickly disconnected from the call.

He dialed the last phone number they had. "Sally Hanover? What would it be worth to you to have a picture of James Hollander's new face and to know when and where he plans to leave the country?"

MILO BUCHANAN SNAPPED to attention at the obvious alarm in his caller's voice. "Calm down. You're talking so fast I can't understand you. Now, who called you?''

''I don't know who it was, but the gist of the conversation was that Hollander has had plastic surgery and plans to leave the country in a couple of days. I'm supposed to decide how much his new identity is worth and wait for another call. What do you think?''

''When did you get this call?''

''Just a little while ago, maybe fifteen minutes.''

Buchanan leaned back in his chair. ''I think someone is playing with your head, trying to run a scam.''

''But what if it's true? What if he's had plastic surgery?''

''It doesn't matter. Even if he does have a new face, there's no way he could hide his identity from me.'' The bitterness crept into Milo Buchanan's voice. ''That man has been a thorn in my side, the bane of my existence for five years. I knew it was just a matter of time until he surfaced again. I'd recognize him anywhere—the way he walks, the way he talks, the sound of his voice, his mannerisms.''

STEVE DIALED THE NUMBER for the pager, then punched in the number of his cellular phone. A few minutes later his phone rang.

''Benny, we've hit a little snag in the plans. I need to be on an eleven o'clock flight out of Los Angeles. I'm afraid we're going to have to move the time of tonight's meeting. We have to move it up to eight o'clock. We'll still use the same location. I assume you'll be able to arrange everything without any problems?''

Benny's voice told of his nervousness. ''I don't like

none of this. Too many people gonna be around earlier in the evening.''

"Not at the location we used last time. Everyone will have been off work for at least a couple of hours. It will be just as deserted as it was the last time.''

"Yeah, I can do that.'' A bit of anxiousness crept into his voice. "You've got my money, right?''

"Don't worry, Benny. We'll take care of you. You just make sure your end of things goes off as planned. I'll check back with you—'' he glanced at his watch "—in a couple of hours.''

As soon as Steve finished his conversation with Benny, he made another call.

"Everything okay on your end, sweetheart?'' Steve leaned back across the bed in his motel room, his manner becoming a little more relaxed than when he talked to Benny.

"I got it, Steve. I found that third numbered account and it's a whopper, the largest of the three.'' The elation in her voice was unmistakable. "The dollar figure for the three accounts totals even more than you thought. It's just a shade under twelve million.''

A low whistle of appreciation escaped his lips. "Wow! I thought it would be somewhere close to ten million, but nearly twelve million...what a bonus. Are you ready to do the transfer as soon as the flight is in the air?''

"Yes, I've already set it up in the computer as an automatic timed transaction to take place ten minutes after the scheduled departure time of the flight. That puts it in the time frame when all phones and computers have to be turned off, so there's no way they can check until after it's done.''

Steve allowed a soft chuckle. "And by then it will

be too late." The grin faded and his voice took on a more serious tone. "At least your part is going off as planned. I've got problems elsewhere. In fact—" he glanced at his watch again "—I have another call to make, then I need to get something to eat before heading for La Jolla."

He quickly terminated this phone conversation, then placed another call, this one to Phil Herman's cellular phone.

"Where are you right now?"

"I'm at the Denver airport. They're just starting boarding for my flight. Everything's on schedule, so I should be arriving on time. What's the problem?"

"Hollander's giving me problems. And what's worse is that now Andi's stirred up and beginning to question things. I still don't know where they were last night. He's demanding a face-to-face meet today. He says he wants some concrete answers or else he's walking."

"What do you plan to do about it?"

"I told him I'd be there by lunch."

"You don't think there's any danger of him deciding to take off before you get there, do you? If there's any chance, then it might be wise to have her house secured. Without him we've got nothing." Phil's comments only gave voice to Steve's unspoken concerns.

"I think he'll stay put until I get there, otherwise there wouldn't have been any reason for him to make the demands. He would have just taken off instead." Steve spoke the words with a positive tone to his voice, however his inner thoughts were not as firmly entrenched.

"Well, I just got another little piece of information to add to our puzzle. Theo Gunzleman."

"Yeah? You were able to find him?" So much had happened in the past couple of days that Steve had almost forgotten about the conversation concerning Theo's current location.

"Sort of. He was killed almost four years ago—drowned at a lake during a Fourth of July celebration."

"Is that confirmed?"

"Yes."

"I don't you were able to find that." Steve's voice had
lapsed in the first couple of days that Steve had
almost forgotten about the conversation concerning
Theos' current interests.

"Son of Jib was killed about four years ago—
drowned in what's called a flash of liquid nitrogen?"
"Is that confirmed?"

Chapter Twelve

"All right, I'm here. Now, what did you want to discuss?" Steve turned to face Jim as Andi closed the
front door.

Jim studied Steve for a minute before speaking.
Whatever thoughts were going through Steve's head
were expertly hidden behind that nondescript facade of
his.

Jim did not waste any time in polite conversation.
"I want to know exactly where you've been and what
you've been doing while we were left here to fend for
ourselves with no knowledge of your plans. Maybe
Andi is accustomed to this type of behavior from you,
but I'm not. I don't know you and so far you haven't
done anything to instill any trust in me. You seem to
have a constant flow of incoming information, very little of which you have chosen to share with me. My
suitcase is packed and I'm ready to leave here right
now unless I get some satisfactory answers." Jim blatantly looked Steve up and down. "And I don't think
you will be able to physically restrain me unless you
have some help standing on the front porch."

Steve took his time pouring a cup of coffee and carrying it into the living room. He pulled aside the drape covering the living room window and looked out at the street, noting the cars parked at the curb, the motor home in the driveway of the newly rented house, and the two boys riding their bicycles.

He finally turned toward Jim, his voice calm and very matter-of-fact. "We seem to have an impasse here. I'm supposed to trust you with all my contacts, with people who need to have their identity protected just as you do, along with my means of gathering information, but you don't want to trust me to know what I'm doing."

It was not at all the answer Jim was looking for. He leveled a long, cool look at Steve. "This has nothing to do with how well you do your job. As near as I can tell, no one on your end is literally gambling with their life, yet that's what you want me to do. You want me to put my life on the line on nothing more than blind faith that something positive is going to happen. I'm not even sure what it is you're trying to accomplish anymore. Ross Durant is dead. An informant has hinted that there's someone connected with all this who is also on Buchanan's payroll. On the basis of that very iffy bit of information, I'm hiding inside a beach house in La Jolla once again constantly looking over my shoulder while Milo Buchanan's day is business as usual without a hint of inconvenience."

"Give me twelve more hours. By that time everything will be over." It was more than Steve wanted to say, but he could see it in Jim's eyes and hear it in his tone of voice—he had to say something definitive to satisfy Jim or be prepared to attempt to physically restrain him. Jim was about three inches taller, ten years younger and in much better shape. Jim had been correct. There was no way Steve could overpower him.

Having Jim as an adversary rather than an ally would not do anyone any good.

"Exactly what is it that will be over?" Jim was not buying the words on face value. He wanted more than just a blanket statement that did not have any meaning or teeth to it.

"Your need to hide away and constantly look over your shoulder to see who's behind you."

Jim still had a very uneasy feeling inside him. Steve's words could have several different meanings, not the least of which was that dead people no longer had any worries. He looked at Andi, at the anxiety on her face and the tenderness in her eyes. Once again it was not his own safety that was uppermost in his mind. Even though he knew that leaving was the most prudent thing to do, he reluctantly followed his heart rather than his head. He swallowed down any further objections and allowed a sigh of resignation. "Twelve more hours, but not a minute longer."

Andi stepped into the awkward silence that followed the exchange between Jim and Steve. "I was about to fix something for lunch. Have you eaten yet, Steve?"

"Yes, I had something a little while ago—sort of a late breakfast. I have to go. I have an appointment in forty-five minutes down the road in San Diego."

Jim's head snapped around at this latest disclosure. "An appointment? So, you're taking off and leaving us alone again. And this appointment is with whom?"

Steve's answer was immediate. "All of my business on the West Coast does not revolve around you. I have another investigation that I'm working on, something I was involved with before Andi called me from Vancouver Island to announce that she had stumbled across the long-missing James Hollander. I can't talk to you about what else I'm working on any more than I can talk about you to someone else not connected with this. I'll be back in about three hours, in plenty of time to discuss the details of tonight's meeting with Benny. So, if you'll let me get on with my business..."

There did not seem to be anything else to say. Jim and Andi watched as Steve got into his car and drove down the street.

Steve drove directly to the San Diego airport. Timing would be tight for the rest of the day. He had to be back at Andi's house no later than four o'clock. He glanced at his watch. The flight was due in at one-thirty. He hoped it was on time.

He parked his car in the short-term parking and made his way to the gate just as the ramp extended out to the plane. A few minutes later Phil Herman exited the plane.

The two men shook hands. "Good to see you, Phil. How was the flight?" They walked quickly through the airport and headed toward the parking lot.

"Not exactly a direct flight—Chicago to New York yesterday under my own name, then leaving New York very early this morning for Denver under an assumed name, with a plane change in Denver along with another name change before continuing on to San Diego."

"I know how easy it is to tap into airline passenger records. We couldn't take a chance on someone picking up on your travels. Is everything set on your end?"

"Yes. I need to go over some last-minute details, but all else is in place. What about the money?"

"I had to spread ten thousand around in dummy packets so that it would look like twenty thousand dollars."

Phil stopped walking and turned toward Steve, the surprise on his face obvious. "What twenty thousand dollars? I thought it was supposed to be ten thousand."

"It was, then that weasel Benny decided to go into business for himself and he hit Andi up for another ten thousand for the name of someone else besides Durant. Sounds to me like he's planning to go into hiding as soon as he gets his hands on the cash...assuming that he lives long enough."

Steve drove Phil to the motel in San Diego where he had been staying. Not only was it close to Andi's house and Jim Hollander, it was away from the Los Angeles airport area should anyone attempt a computer check of registered guests. He had made arrangements for a car for Phil, not wanting Phil's name to show up on any car rental records. Phil took the car and the two men went their separate ways, each to take care of last-minute details. Time was growing short. As Steve had said, everything would soon be all over.

Steve took care of his loose ends and made it back to Andi's house by five minutes after four. He was right on schedule. The next step would be tricky, but he considered it necessary. He had to separate Jim and Andi. He took a steadying breath and walked up to the front door. As soon as he stepped up on the porch, the door swung open with Andi standing on the other side.

"Could you step out here for a moment, Andi? I need to talk to you in private. There's something I need to have you do for me."

Andi cocked her head and leveled a quizzical look at him. She hesitated a moment, then stepped out onto the porch. They walked out into the front yard away from the house.

"Rollie is flying in to San Diego in connection with

this other investigation I'm working on. I was supposed to pick him up at the airport, but Jim's so concerned about my comings and goings that I thought it might be better if I stayed here until it was time to drive up to Los Angeles for the meeting with Benny. So, I need to have you pick him up for me.''

"Me?" Her surprise was evident.

"It's either you or me, and I think, under the circumstances, that I need to stay where Jim can keep his eye on me. He seems to be very uncomfortable with my absences. You know Rollie and he knows you. He'll accept your word that I sent you where he wouldn't give some stranger the time of day. So, unless you want to go through another bout of Jim's insecurities—" He saw the flicker of anger that darted through her eyes and knew he should not have worded it in that manner.

"Jim's insecurities? That's a rather harsh indictment, wouldn't you say? I think his anxieties are perfectly understandable and his caution is well-founded."

"It was a bad choice of words. Of course he's entitled to his concerns. But, back to Rollie. His flight lands in an hour and I need for you to rent a motel room for him before that.'' Steve took some money from his pocket and handed it to her. "Pay cash for the room for one night and give Rollie this one hundred dollars for expense money. Tell him I'll see him in the morning.''

"But what about our meeting with Benny?"

"You should be back in plenty of time before we need to leave for Los Angeles.'' Steve extended a confident smile. "You'd better get going. You know how nervous Rollie gets if things don't happen the way he's expecting them to.''

Andi glanced at her watch. There would be plenty of time. "Okay. I'll get my car keys."

She entered her house with Steve behind her. Jim threw a suspicious look toward Steve, then addressed his comments to Andi. "What's going on?"

She reached out for his hand and smiled at him. "It's nothing. I need to go to the San Diego airport. I'll be back in a little while. Steve's going to keep you company while I'm gone."

She reached her face up to his and placed a loving kiss on his lips. Her words were soft, intended for Jim's ears only. "Just a few short hours and all of this will be behind us for good."

Jim watched in silence as Andi gathered her keys and purse and walked through the kitchen door into the garage. He heard the garage door open and her car start. A minute later she was gone. A sudden jolt of trepidation hit him, a feeling that he might never see Andi again. A premonition of some sort? Possibly. But exactly who was the person in danger, Andi or himself? He did not know.

He turned his attention to Steve. "What's this little errand you have Andi doing?"

"Nothing that has anything to do with this. It's that other investigation I mentioned earlier. She's just doing an errand, then she'll meet us at the location where we're meeting Benny." He waited for what he knew would be an adverse reaction from Jim.

"She's going to meet us there?" Jim definitely did not like the sound of that. "I thought you said it was a quick errand. It's only four-thirty and we aren't due to be there until tonight."

"Not exactly…" Steve shifted his weight from one foot to the other. This was going to take all of his persuasive powers. "The meeting has been moved up to eight o'clock. What with the traffic, we need to leave here in the next ten or fifteen minutes."

Jim leveled a hard look at Steve. "We're leaving before Andi gets back?" He tried to hold down his anger, but it was not working. "What are you trying to pull? What's really going on here?"

Steve paused for a moment, as if turning something over in his mind. "All right, here's the deal. Milo Buchanan himself is going to be there." He saw the look of shock dart across Jim's face. "This is our one and only chance to get him into a compromising position and nail him with personal involvement."

Total disbelief colored Jim's tone of voice. "Are you trying to tell me that Milo Buchanan is actually getting on a plane and leaving Chicago to fly to Los Angeles for the purpose of meeting in some dark alley by the airport?" Jim spit out the words. "Give it a rest, Steve. You don't really expect me to buy that, do you?"

Jim made a quick move toward the bedroom and emerged with his suitcase in his hand. The hint of surprise that crossed Steve's face in response to his already-packed suitcase provided a bit of self-satisfaction for Jim, but he did not allow it to show. He was pleased to have found at least one thing that Steve did not already know about. "You've been running me around in circles from day one. I don't know what your game is—"

Jim paused a moment as he looked curiously at Steve. "Maybe you're the one who has the ties to Buchanan. You say good ol' Milo is going to be here personally? I guess he insisted on looking me over himself to make sure it's really me, something you can't guarantee him because you've never met the real Jim Hollander. Is that it, Steve?''

Steve's face was set in grim determination. Gone was the nondescript expression and the easily forgettable persona. His eyes darkened and conveyed a hard look. His tone of voice became intense, his words emphatic. "I want this guy. I wanted him five years ago and I want him now. Milo Buchanan has to pay for all the damage he's done and all the lives he's endangered. I was hoping to get him back into court on the original charges, but now that I know about that second attempt on your life I think we can get him on the much more serious charge of conspiracy to commit murder, even without Ross Durant.''

Jim was not exactly sure how to respond to what he had just seen and heard. He did not like the Steve Westerfall he had known over the past few days. And now he had been given an unexpected glimpse into the real character of this top investigative reporter. As much as he did not want to, he had to reluctantly admit that he was impressed. It was not so much what he had said or his obvious change in demeanor, but the dedication attached to the way he had said it.

Steve opened the door and stepped out onto the porch. "Let's go. We have a date with destiny." He gave a self-conscious chuckle and added, "If that doesn't sound too cornball." The two men walked to Steve's car and a minute later were headed toward the freeway. It was not quite five o'clock.

They rode along for a while in silence, each of them lost in their own thoughts. It was Jim who broke the silence.

"Why are you so intent on putting Buchanan behind bars? You made it sound almost as if it were a personal vendetta of some sort rather than something for the good of the community in general or an attempt to right a wrong, or even just a good news story.''

"Why am I so set on nailing Buchanan, no matter what? Well...I guess *personal vendetta* is as good a description as any. It has to do with my nephew.'' Steve took a steadying breath. He did not like telling the story, but he felt it necessary under the circumstances.

"One of Buchanan's dump sites was a creek that ran through a wooded area next to a new housing development where my sister and her family lived. They had just moved in and Johnny was exploring through the woods behind the house. He found the little creek and thought it would be a great place to play. He was eight years old. It was two years later when you blew the whistle on Buchanan. A year and a half after that Johnny was dead from cancer caused by the toxic witch's brew that Buchanan had dumped into that creek. Johnny was just a couple of months away from his twelfth birthday when he died.''

Jim had not known what to expect, but this certainly was not it. Steve's eyes seemed to be focused on some place far away, but his pain still showed. Jim's words were soft and sincere. "I'm sorry. I didn't know.''

"Five years ago, when you disappeared and Milo Buchanan went free, you shot up to the top of my hit list with only Buchanan ahead of you. My first thought, my only thought about it, was that you had been bought off. I wanted you almost as bad as I wanted Buchanan.''

Jim stiffened to attention. "Wait just a damn minute. No way—''

"Settle down. Now that I know what happened, I

can honestly say I'd have done the same thing you did.'' Steve paused again in an attempt to force a sense of calm. ''And now things have come full circle. Tonight we nail Buchanan and see that he's put away this time. It may have taken five years, but it'll be done. He won't get away from us—I promise you.''

Jim leaned back in the bucket seat as he assimilated what he had just heard. He slowly nodded as he allowed a bittersweet smile, everything now making sense. ''And I'm your bait. The only thing important enough to get Milo Buchanan to tip his hand and become personally involved is the opportunity for him to get at me…an opportunity he can't afford to pass up no matter how risky. Since he had allowed underlings to handle it before with unsatisfactory results, this time he would insist on overseeing things in person. I must say, you seem to have done a masterful job of manipulating everything and everyone.''

Suddenly his heart felt very heavy. His voice filled with the despair that flooded through his reality. ''And what was Andi's part in all of this? Was she responsible for seeing that I'd stay put so I'd be here when you needed me?''

Steve did not answer his question. Both men lapsed into silence.

ANDI HAD ONLY GOTTEN about ten minutes away from home on her trip to the San Diego airport. Thoughts kept running through her mind, things that did not fit together. Something was wrong, very wrong. Why would Steve have Rollie fly out to California? In fact, the more she thought about it, she seemed to remember Steve telling her that one of the conditions of Rollie's parole was that he could not leave the state of New

York. And even if she was mistaken about that, why have him fly into San Diego the same evening that Steve would be right next to the Los Angeles airport?

A sudden surge of panic jabbed her. It was a ruse. For some reason Steve had sent her on a wild-goose chase. But why? Her car tires squealed as she expertly spun the car around in a U-turn. She shoved her foot against the accelerator and sped back to her house. She charged into her driveway and screeched to a halt just short of hitting the garage door. Steve's car was gone. She ran up the porch steps, unlocked the front door and burst into the living room.

"Jim...are you here?" She rushed to the back and threw open the French doors. "Jim...are you out here?" She raced across the yard and looked down at the beach, calling out his name one more time. No response...nothing. She returned to the house. What had happened? Had Jim and Steve gone somewhere together? A note...he probably left her a note.

Andi froze in her tracks when she spotted the man standing just inside her front door. A twinge of foreboding shivered across her nape as her heart pounded. She swallowed down her fear and took a step backward, feeling behind her for the handle to the French door.

"Don't be alarmed, Miss Sinclair. You're not in any danger."

She tried to force a confident tone to her words. "Who are you? How did you know my name?"

"Steve Westerfall put my partner and me here. He had us rent the house across the street so we could keep an eye on things and make sure everyone was safe."

Her anxieties lessened a little, but she remained on

alert and did not move away from her avenue of escape. "Where are Steve and Jim?"

"Steve left right after you did. He said he'd be back in a couple of hours and wanted you to wait for him. I'm not sure about Jim. We asked him to stay in the house, but he said he wanted to go for a walk along the beach. Apparently that's what he decided to do. I'm sure he'll be back soon."

"Well...okay. Thanks for letting me know." She remained by the French doors.

The man did not seem to be quite sure about what to do next. He shuffled his feet awkwardly for a moment. "Uh...I'm just across the street at the house with the motor home parked in the driveway. If you need anything, just signal, I'll be watching." He left the house and went back across the street.

Andi rushed to the front door and slammed it shut. She leaned back against it as she assimilated this new bit of information. So, Steve had not left them unprotected after all. She felt a little better, however it did not explain where Jim had gone. She looked for a note, but did not find one. Something was still wrong. She went outside, crossed the lawn and opened the back gate. She stood at the top of the steps and looked up and down the beach, straining to see if she could find him. Then it hit her. The tide had recently gone out. The sand was wet within a few feet of the bottom of the steps. There were no footprints. No one had been on the beach.

Whoever that man was, he had lied to her. Had he really been sent by Steve? She ran through the house and out to the front yard. Her gaze raked up and down the street until she spotted what she hoped she would find—Nick's car. She raced toward it.

Her urgency sounded as loudly as her words. "Nick, how long have you been here?"

Concern quickly darted across his features. "I arrived just as you were driving down the street. What's the matter? Is something wrong?"

"I'm sure...I'm not sure. Did you see Steve leave?"

"Yes. He and that other guy left together in Steve's car about fifteen minutes ago."

"Steve and Jim left together?" She was not sure what she felt—anger, concern, confusion or relief—but whatever it was she did not like it. She turned around and stared toward the rental house, trying to will her gaze to penetrate through the wall so she could see what was going on inside.

Nick's voice took on an added edge of distress. "Is everything okay? Is there anything I can do?"

"Damn!" A total realization of what had happened exploded in her mind with amazing clarity. They had gone to Los Angeles to meet with Benny. Somehow Steve had managed to move up the time and had sent her in the opposite direction while they headed north. Jim was unprotected. She did not know what Steve was up to or even what good she could do, but she suddenly felt very afraid for Jim.

She returned to her house, grabbed her car keys and purse and ran back out, slamming the door behind her. She shot one more quick glance toward the rental house with the motor home in the driveway. Had they been following Steve's instructions? Telling her to just wait until everyone came back? Well, she was not buying it. Hopefully Steve had not changed the location of the meet.

She had to set her anxieties and anger aside, they would only cloud her thinking. She jumped in her car and drove down the street toward the freeway. They did not have that much of a head start on her. For most of the way she would be going the opposite direction of the main traffic flow for that time of evening. If she hit it lucky, she could be there in a couple of hours.

THE THREE PASSENGERS exited the nonstop Chicago to Los Angeles flight. Gordon went first, his large size easily clearing a way for the two people following him. They picked up their rental car, checked into a hotel by the airport, then sat down to plan the evening's work.

Milo Buchanan lit one of his cigars. "I'm unhappy with the phone call I received from Benny right before we left for the airport. This moving up of the meeting time at the last minute...I'm very concerned about what it could mean. Benny didn't seem to have any specific information about it, just that if we wanted to see Hollander that's when we needed to be there. You put that together with the other last-minute phone call from the *mysterious stranger* who claimed Hollander had plastic surgery and was leaving the country...well, I don't like it. Something strange is going on here that I don't know about."

Gordon tried to answer his boss's concerns. "Gee, I don't know, Mr. Buchanan. Do you think Benny was giving us some bad stuff? He's played pretty straight with me in the past. Of course, this was kind of different from what we usually have him do."

"I think it would be wise if you had a little chat with him, Gordon. Make sure he understands our philosophy of doing business, especially if he wants to do any business with us in the future...assuming that he has a future."

The third member of the group finally voiced some personal concerns. "For crying out loud, Milo. You can't go around bashing everyone who annoys you. I don't even know why we're here. You want to eliminate Hollander? Why couldn't you just have Gordon here do it, or better yet hire it out to someone local? I think this is much too great a risk, you and I here at all, let alone together. What if someone spots us? In fact, I don't know why you need me here at all. There's nothing I can contribute to this little *endeavor* of yours."

"You think it's too much of a risk?" Milo took a deep draw on the cigar and slowly expelled the smoke. "Where do you think you will be if Hollander is able to put the finger on me?"

It was a question that went unanswered, in fact did not even require an answer.

Milo rose from his chair and crossed to the window. The last streaks of sunset faded from the sky as the city lights dominated more and more of the landscape. "There is a very specific reason for your presence. I'll be face-to-face with Hollander. I have to see him, hear his voice. I want to make sure it's really him. He will be on his guard. Gordon here will need to be with me so that Hollander can keep his eye on both of us. It will keep his attention focused and he'll think he has control of the situation. I'll offer him money to leave the country immediately, something to help him get established wherever he's going. While he's busy with us you'll be able to get him in your sights without him suspecting that anything is amiss."

Milo nodded toward Gordon, who produced a handgun and placed it on the table. "You won't be more than thirty feet away at the most. You won't have any trouble hitting your target."

"Me?" Total shock and an extremely high stress level jumped into the response. "You want me to shoot him? Are you crazy? I'm not a hired killer. I work at a desk. I've never shot anyone in my life! What makes you think I even know to shoot this thing?"

A hard look crossed Milo's face. "Don't play me for a fool, not after all these years. I know everything there is to know about my associates. I know you went to the gun range for target practice last month." He shoved the gun across the table. "Let's just call this *my* insurance policy."

Milo straightened up and glanced at his watch. "Another hour and it will all be over."

Chapter Thirteen

Jim and Steve traveled north from San Diego County, through Orange County and into Los Angeles County, headed toward the airport before there was any more conversation.

"So, what happens now?" Jim's question was addressed to Steve, but his thoughts were on Andi. Exactly where did her loyalties lie? And did she know about the change in the time of the meeting with Benny or that Milo Buchanan would be there?

"We meet Benny at the same place, only at eight o'clock rather than midnight. He's expecting twenty thousand dollars in exchange for the name of Buchanan's other inside man. He also thinks he's going to walk away free and clear."

"And is he?"

"Maybe yes and maybe no. It's up to what Milo Buchanan has planned for him."

This little bit of information grabbed Jim's attention. The disbelief in his voice was edged out by the irritation. "Are you telling me after all of this that Benny is one of Milo Buchanan's people? Since you were apparently able to get in touch with him and in a position to exercise enough authority to change the time of the meeting, I had assumed that he was one of your people. In fact—'' Jim turned sideways to look directly at Steve ''—it seems to me that this entire setup of Joey finding Benny, who claimed to have information for sale, was just that...a contrived setup. It makes me wonder exactly who got in touch with whom. Perhaps you engineered this entire thing for the purpose of getting information to Milo Buchanan that said you could supply my presence. Is that what happened or would you care to tell me exactly how Benny fits into this?''

''Benny is a minor-league crook and an informant for whoever has the money to pay him. He has a nasty little habit of liking to play both ends against the middle. He never really knows enough to get himself into much trouble...until now. I'd guess that Buchanan has no idea about Benny putting the squeeze on Andi for an additional ten grand and hinting at another inside person.''

''And I suppose you already know who this other insider is? Or would it be more accurate to say that there isn't anyone else?''

''There's someone, all right. I've suspected for a long time and now I know.''

''So what do you need me for? Tell what you know to the police and they can arrest this person. Then they can get the information they need to arrest Milo Buchanan.''

''The fact that I know the other person's identity is not the same thing as proof.''

Steve took the airport exit off the freeway, then turned onto a dark side street. Even though they were only two blocks from a main thoroughfare, the street was deserted and the buildings dark. Jim recognized it as the same area where they had met with Benny the first time.

The tingle of anxiety nudged at his nerves and slowly spread through his body. Steve had revealed some of what had been going on behind his back, but he knew there was more that Steve was not telling him. He also knew that he was still nothing more than bait, a means to an end for Steve Westerfall. The only saving grace was that Steve's ultimate goal seemed to be the same as Jim's—to put Milo Buchanan behind bars. And Steve had the contacts to pull it off. Jim never would have been able to accomplish it on his own. But that did not change his negative opinion of Steve's tactics.

Steve pulled into an alley, turned off his headlights and drove to the end of the block. He parked next to the building in the same spot where they had originally met with Benny. He turned off the engine and leaned back in the seat, making no effort to get out of the car.

"We're about fifteen minutes early. The meeting will take place over there—" Steve indicated the entrance to a walkway between buildings "—just like last time. We can keep our eye on the spot to make sure things are on the up-and-up."

"I've got another tiny little question." Again, Jim made no effort to hide his sarcasm. "If Buchanan plans to be here in person, what does he think he's going to accomplish? He tried to buy me off once before and it didn't work. Surely he wouldn't be trying that again."

"I don't know…you have been on the run for five years. He might figure that you're wanting to leave the country and would now be willing to accept the money."

A little twinge of discomfort tugged at Jim's senses.

Was it only coincidence or did Steve know about the phone calls he and Andi had made that morning about Jim Hollander having plastic surgery and leaving the country? "So, we're just going to sit here and do nothing until someone else shows up?"

"Yes, that's basically it. Until we see Benny we don't get out of the car."

Jim shifted his weight awkwardly in his seat. The total reality of what was about to happen settled over him. The worrying and uncertainty had just come to a screeching halt. In a matter of minutes everything would be out in the open...including himself. He had to focus his attention on practical and serious matters.

"If Buchanan has his gunman with him, then shouldn't I at least have some sort of bulletproof vest to wear...or is that a little detail that you overlooked since it didn't apply directly to you?" Jim knew the accusation and sarcasm were blatantly obvious and inappropriate, but at this point he was about at the end of his rope. He had been pushed, shoved, manipulated and used. All he wanted at that moment was for it to all be over. It was do or die...a choice he hoped he had some control over.

Jim continued to stare at the spot where they would be meeting. "And while I'm asking questions, other than the fact that you're sitting here in the car with me, what steps have you taken to safeguard this entire meeting? It's not like the last one. As you said, they couldn't afford to make any moves against anyone then until they knew for sure where I was hiding. Well, the guessing game is over and here I am." When Jim did not get an immediate response to his concerns, he turned toward Steve.

Something had grabbed Steve's attention. He had directed his gaze down the street toward the corner. Jim followed the line of sight and saw a dark sedan round the corner and drive slowly down the street toward them. The car with its single occupant did not slow as it continued past their location.

Steve indicated the car's retreating taillights. "That's your answer. The two men who moved into the rental house across from Andi were put there by me. One of them stayed behind to be there when Andi got home and the other one just drove down the street. So, you can see there really isn't any need for all that concern."

Jim was not convinced. "One guy in a car? That's it?"

"Buchanan is so obsessed with you that he's falling all over himself making mistakes. Everything he's done since that blurb about Andi's book appeared has been sloppy and not thought out at all—very uncharacteristic of his normally meticulous nature. He may seem cool on the outside, but right now he's totally out of control on the inside. He's reacting to everything emotionally rather than taking the time to figure things out logically, and that gives us a very big edge. He's left an easy trail to follow. What's even more surprising is that he's allowed Gordon to use his heavy-handed techniques to accomplish things that should have had a much more delicate touch—"

"Such as breaking into Keith Martin's office and ransacking Andi's house?"

"Exactly."

"That's all well and good, but it doesn't answer my concern about Buchanan shooting me as soon as he sets eyes on me."

"To the best of my knowledge, he hasn't contacted any local people. He has Gordon with him. He can't depend on Benny for anything. Benny will cut and run the second he gets his hands on the briefcase with what he assumes is his twenty thousand dollars—''

''*Assumes* is his twenty thousand?''

Steve clenched his jaw as he shook his head. ''Ten was all I could get. I wasn't prepared for Benny to hit us up for another ten. He's never been that brave before, which is what makes me think he plans to go into hiding, especially with what happened to Durant.''

Steve continued with his explanation of what he had arranged. ''My man will have Gordon and Buchanan covered. He'll situate himself in a second-floor window—'' Steve indicated the building next to where they had parked ''—as soon as he finishes cruising the neighborhood. And you won't be out there alone. I'll be right beside you.''

''You're getting out of the car?'' There was no missing the total surprise in Jim's voice.

''Yes. I have a briefcase of money to deliver. Besides, it will help keep Gordon and Buchanan busy if they need to worry about why I'm there or who I am, in case they don't already know. There's nothing to be concerned about. In less than an hour we'll be on our way back to La Jolla.''

''Why can't you contact the local police? Buchanan's not under investigation for anything in California. There isn't any reason for the local law enforcement or prosecution personnel to be in his pocket.''

''That's right, as far as it goes. But as you said, he isn't under investigation in California. There hasn't been any crime committed within the state of California that would allow the local authorities to become involved. As soon as we start talking about the original Federal charges or the local office of the FBI, U.S.

Marshals or the U.S. Attorneys office is notified, that could provide a pipeline directly back to Buchanan.''

Jim digested Steve's words. It all made sense. There was no mistaking nor any way to minimize what they both knew was the danger Jim would be in, but the end result would be worth the risk. At least one thing was for certain. Regardless of what her part was in all of this, Andi was safely away from what was about to happen.

Jim regarded the determined expression on Steve's face as he let out a sigh of resignation. His voice was soft and his words reflective. ''You know, not once during all of this have you ever asked me how much I would be willing to risk. You've pushed, shoved, manipulated and made my decisions for me—which I have to admit I've allowed you to do—but never once did you ask me.''

''I'm not expecting you to do anything I'm not willing to do myself. If someone starts shooting, I'll be in the line of fire every bit as much as you are.''

Steve turned toward Jim, cocked his head and allowed a hint of a grin. ''Does that make you feel better?''

Jim returned the grin, breaking the tension that had existed between the two men from the moment they first met. ''Yes, it does make me feel a little better.''

Any further discussion came to an abrupt halt when a car pulled up to the curb on the other side of the street. The door on the passenger side opened and a large man stepped out. The driver's door opened and Benny quickly got out and ran around the front of the car to the sidewalk. The large man opened the back door and a slight man with gray hair exited.

Steve looked at Jim, took a steadying breath and reached for the door handle. "It's time."

Major anxiety churned in the pit of Jim's stomach—anxiety and fear. Very real danger permeated the air. He could almost smell it. There was no point in his denying it—he was scared. When the car bomb put him in the hospital and then someone made yet another attempt on his life, the unexpected happenings had exploded around him without warning.

This was different. The total reality of the extreme danger had covered him like a blanket for the past few hours. He was walking into this with his eyes wide open and full knowledge of what could happen. He felt an adrenaline rush as he tried to swallow down his trepidation. His heart pounded hard inside his chest. He swung his long legs out the passenger side of the car as Steve exited from the driver's side.

Both men paused for a moment. Steve passed on one last bit of information. "We'll be sort of winging it from here. What we say and do depends on what Buchanan does."

Jim nodded his head to acknowledge that he understood, then the two men walked out of the shadows and away from the protection of the car and building. They stepped off the curb and started across the street.

The air hung thick and still with the only sounds being a distant hum of traffic from a few blocks away. Each footstep echoed along the deserted street and down the alley. A shadowy figure situated himself in a recessed doorway about thirty feet down the walkway between the buildings from where Buchanan, Gordon and Benny waited on the street.

But that was not the only unannounced pair of eyes watching the drama unfold.

Andi had parked one block over and hugged the edge of the building, hidden in the shadows as she made her way toward the mouth of the alley were Steve had parked his car. She tried to fight down her fears while forcing all her energy into the task ahead. She did not have a clear-cut idea about what she was going to do, but somehow she had to make sure Jim would be safe. She saw Steve and Jim get out of the car and start across the street. Both of them were out in the open, exposed to whatever danger lurked in the shadows.

She squinted at the three men standing on the other side of the street. The plan had been for her to meet alone with Benny as she had done last time. She recognized Benny, but did not know who the other two men were.

The three men on the other side of the street watched as Steve and Jim crossed toward them. Milo Buchanan leaned toward Benny. "I thought you said this Sinclair woman, the writer, was part of this and that she would be with Hollander. Where is she?"

"I don't know, Mr. Buchanan. She's the one I met with and she's the one I talked to on the phone."

"And tell me, Benny. The other man—is that this reporter fellow? Steve Westerfall?"

"Yeah, that's Westerfall."

"I don't like this change in plans." Buchanan shifted his weight from one foot to the other as he continued to stare at the two men walking toward him. "That certainly does look like James Hollander, and if it is, then he hasn't had any plastic surgery."

Suddenly Milo Buchanan whirled around to face Gordon. "So what was that phone call about, the one talking about him changing his face and leaving the country? I have a bad feeling about this, Gordon. A very bad feeling. I think we might have overlooked something along the way.''

Gordon's response showed his confusion. "I don't know what it would be, Mr. Buchanan. Maybe it meant that he was gonna have a face job after he was out of the country.''

"It really doesn't matter, does it? After all, he probably won't be walking away from here. I offered him money once before and he turned me down flat. I would imagine that will be his reaction again." Milo furrowed his brow for a moment as if in thought. "However, he has been on the run for five years. He's probably tired and broke. There just might be some truth to the call about him wanting to leave the country. We'll soon know.''

"I don't understand what the problem is, Mr. Buchanan. Why would you even want to offer him money again?''

"I guess you could call it a weakness, Gordon. He was an excellent employee who worked hard and was very dependable. Of course, in retrospect it seems that perhaps he worked a bit too hard. I've always liked James and felt badly about what needed to be done, but business was business and sentiment did not have a place. He did manage to survive two attempts on his life, to slip away from his watchdogs before they even knew what happened, and successfully disappeared for five years. I suppose you could say that I'm just reluctant to put an end to someone that resourceful.''

Any further speculation was put on hold as Jim and Steve stepped up on the sidewalk and stopped about five feet away.

A cruel smirk crossed Gordon's face, while a frightened one plastered itself to Benny's countenance. Milo Buchanan appeared to be the master of an expressionless facade.

Jim stared at Buchanan for a moment as if he were surprised to see his old nemesis. He then glared at Steve, indicating that the reality of what was happening had just dawned on him. Without saying a word he turned to leave. It was a little charade that they had not discussed, but it seemed to provide the appropriate impact. Gordon quickly grabbed Jim's arm and brought him to a halt.

Benny gestured toward the briefcase Steve carried. He glanced toward Milo Buchanan as if seeking permission, then returned his attention to Steve. He tentatively reached out for the case.

Steve's voice showed a calm control. He offered a confident smile. "Not so fast, Benny. This is yours, but it's in exchange for the information we discussed."

"Uh…yeah, sure…" Benny glanced at Milo Buchanan, then nervously toward Gordon before he turned back to Steve. "Yeah…the guy…Durant, that's the name." Benny's gaze became riveted to Steve, the fear in his eyes pleading to let it drop at that without mentioning anything else.

Steve wanted Benny out of the way as much as Benny obviously wanted to get away. He forced as much pseudoanger into his voice as he could. "That's it, Benny? All you've got for me is the name of a dead guy?"

"That's all I know…honest." A very nervous Benny grabbed the briefcase from Steve, then took a couple of steps backward.

Steve moved toward Benny as he reached out to take the case back when Gordon placed his hand in the middle of Steve's chest to stop him. Benny took another step farther away and Steve maintained his angry expression.

Milo Buchanan stared at Jim, then a smirk of satisfaction tugged at the corners of his mouth. "Well, James…this has been a long time coming, but we finally meet again. I must admit that you're doing a fair job of hiding your surprise at seeing me, especially considering that you were expecting to get some valuable information from Benny here."

Jim spit out his hostile response. "So…you set me up."

Benny nervously cleared his throat as he glanced at Jim, then back to Milo Buchanan. "Uh…so—I done what I was supposed to. Okay if I go now, Mr. Buchanan? I gotta catch my plane back to Chicago." He began edging away from the group. "I can get my own way to the airport."

"Hold on there, Benny." Milo eyed him suspiciously. "Don't you want to count your money before you leave?"

"Uh…I gotta be goin'." Benny took another step away.

"Not so fast." Gordon's big hand came down on Benny's shoulder. "Mr. Buchanan asked you a question."

Jim felt his eyes widen as the shock jolted through his body, mixed with a hint of excitement. He riveted his hard stare on Gordon. That voice…he knew he would never forget it even though it had been five years. It was the same raspy voice he heard that night when someone had made the second attempt on his life.

Benny stammered out an answer, pulling Jim's attention away from his own thoughts. "No, I…uh…I don't need to count it. I'm …yeah, I'm sure it's okay. I gotta go…don't wanna miss my plane.''

''Certainly, Benny.'' Milo Buchanan made a slight gesture toward Gordon, who immediately took his hand off Benny's shoulder. ''We'll be in touch in a couple of days.''

''Yeah…sure.'' A grateful smile and a sigh of relief were all Benny could muster. He hurried down the street and around the corner. As soon as he was out of sight from the rest of the group, he stopped and opened the briefcase. A shadowy figure stepped out from an opened door, put his hand over Benny's mouth and dragged him inside the building. The door closed without making a sound.

Jim glanced down the street toward the corner where Benny had disappeared. Something strange was going on and he could not quite put his finger on it. Everyone seemed to be waiting for something…but for what? Benny had taken his money and skipped out, just as Steve said he would. It was obvious that nobody was going to name another government employee on Buchanan's payroll. So, what were they doing there?

Jim tried to sort it out in his mind. Steve had used him as bait to lure Buchanan out of the safe environment of Chicago and into California. Had Buchanan used Benny in the same manner? Dangling him in front of Steve like a carrot with the promise of finding out the agent's name in order to see if it would lead to Jim Hollander?

A little shiver of dread tickled across the back of Jim's neck. He fought the strong urge to turn around and look to the second floor of the building across the street to verify that Steve's associate was in place and had the situation covered. He felt so utterly defenseless and totally vulnerable. It was true that he and Steve did have these two men in full view and could attempt to thwart any surreptitious moves on their part.

He did not know about Steve, but he was unarmed, so being in a position to stop any moves did not lessen the apprehension that continued to poke at his consciousness. If Steve had a man hidden away, so could Buchanan. Why in the world had he allowed Steve to talk him into this? Or, more accurately, why had he quietly gone along with some unknown plan devised by Steve Westerfall?

Milo Buchanan put a stop to any further speculation on Jim's part. "If you recall, James, I offered you a great deal of money to go away. You spurned my offer and it cost you dearly." He stared at Jim as if turning something over in his mind. "Perhaps the years have taught you a lesson. I'm willing to make a one-time payment to you if you go straight to the airport and take a flight out of the country. What do you say to that?"

Jim outwardly ignored the omnipresent threat of Gordon even though the intimidation remained very real. He covered his every word in disgust, showing no external fear or apprehension about what might happen. "Do you think for one minute I'm going to believe that you'd just let me walk out of here and get on a plane with your money in my pocket? I didn't want your money then and I don't want it now. What I do want is the same thing I wanted five years ago. I want to see you in jail."

He shot a harsh glare at Gordon. "And that goes for your gorilla here, too." He came within a breath of blurting out that he had recognized Gordon's voice as that belonging to the person who had tried to kill him, but thought better of it at the last second.

Buchanan maintained a calm outer facade. "That's really not a very productive attitude, James. You know you can't win."

For the first time Milo regarded Steve, who had been standing quietly. "Gordon, it occurs to me that this *reporter*—" he spit out the word as if it were poison "—just might be recording what we're saying. See if they are wired or have any hidden recording devices."

As Gordon stepped forward and motioned for Steve and Jim to take off their jackets, Andi gazed up and down the street, searching out a better vantage point. She could not hear much of what they were saying, only catching the occasional word. She wanted to cross the street so that she would be on the same side as they were, but there was no way to do it without being out in the open where everyone could see her.

She took advantage of the fact that everyone seemed to have their attention concentrated on what the large man was doing. She stayed close to the building and ducked back into each recessed doorway as she slowly made her way to the other side of the alley where Steve had parked his car. It would give her a different view from what Jim and Steve had. She would be able to see any activity going on down the walkway behind them in an area hidden from their line of sight.

She spotted the odd gesture Steve made with his left hand when the large man stepped forward and motioned for them to take off their jackets, but did not understand exactly what it was. A signal to someone? She glanced quickly up and down the street. A signal to whom? The large man seemed to be checking Steve and Jim for something. To see if they were armed? No, more likely to see if they were wired.

She continued to watch, uncertain about what to do or what action to take—if any.

Gordon quickly finished checking both men. "They're clean, Mr. Buchanan." He stepped back so that he stood to one side and slightly behind Milo, as if he were a giant robot waiting for the next command.

A hard look crossed Buchanan's face, one tinged with just a hint of genuine regret. "I'm sorry you've decided on this stubborn course of action, James. I truly am sorry." He moved slightly to one side and took a step back, as if distancing himself from Jim and Steve. A signal of some sort? Jim was not sure.

Another shiver of fear rippled across Jim's skin as he nervously eyed Gordon, alert to any move or gesture. The anxiety churned in the pit of his stomach. He could feel it in the air. He could almost taste it. Whatever was going to happen would erupt any moment.

Chapter Fourteen

Even from across the street Andi could feel the tension in the air. She watched the small man shift position, then the large man follow suit and take a step away from Jim and Steve. The adrenaline rush jumped her heartbeat into high gear as it pounded in her chest. She did not know what to do. She desperately wanted to run across the street and be with Jim, but she knew it was not a wise thing to do. She could not take a chance on barging into the middle of whatever scenario Steve was playing out.

Her gaze darted up and down the street, searching for anything that seemed out of place. She quickly returned her attention to the group of men across the street. Then she saw a movement in the shadows back in the walkway behind Jim and Steve. At least she thought she saw something. She blinked, squinted and attempted to focus clearly as she stared into the darkened walkway. She saw it again. Then she froze as fear lodged in her throat. It was a man with a gun at an angle where Jim and Steve could not see him.

A curtain descended over her consciousness. All logic and practicality disappeared from her reality. Someone with a gun had taken aim at Jim and she had to put a stop to it. She did not have any clear-cut plan or even a thought about exactly what to do. Her feet started moving, at first slowly as she stepped out of the protection of the doorway. She took a couple of more steps, then broke into a run headed straight toward Jim and Steve.

She opened her mouth, but it went dry and nothing came out. Then she heard her own voice. It sounded shrill, as if it belonged to someone else, coming from some other place. "Jim...*Jim!*"

She ran faster, each step pounding hard against the pavement. She quickly closed the distance between them until she was only ten feet away from him. "Look out behind you!"

She reached him just as he stepped aside and turned toward her. At that same moment the shot rang out. Andi felt the searing pain rip into her, felt herself falling, then being caught in someone's arms. She looked up into Jim's face and saw his stunned expression and the terror that clouded his eyes.

"Andi. Andi!" All the color had drained from her face, leaving it ashen. The horror flooded through him when he saw the blood spread across her jacket. He could not keep his fear out of his voice. "Say something, Andi. Talk to me. Are you all right?" He closed his eyes. His whispered words came out almost as a thought that had managed to escape into the open. "Don't die on me, Andi. Don't you dare die on me."

Exactly what had happened? He'd heard her shout, turned toward her, and the next thing he knew he had her body cradled in his arms as her blood stained her clothes. His voice quavered as he tried to shove down his panic and project an air of calm, as much if not more for her benefit as his own. "Talk to me, Andi. Are you okay? Where were you hit?"

Her words came out in a thin gasp. "My shoulder. I think…I guess I'm okay." She tried to force a bit of a smile. "No vital organs in the shoulder…are there?"

He did not realize he had been holding his breath until he finally expelled it. She would be all right. An incredible wave of relief swept over Jim, shoving everything else from his mind, including the fact that whoever had fired the shot was still hiding somewhere—and that he had just turned his back on Gordon and Milo Buchanan. Somewhere in an obscure corner of his mind, he heard Steve shout something, but all his attention was focused on Andi.

"This will probably hurt a little bit. I'm going to move you over to this doorway so you can sit up and won't be in the middle of everything. Here we go." Jim picked her up and gently placed her with her back against the door. He took off his jacket and started to tuck it around her when a chilling reality in the form of Buchanan's voice reached his ears and brought him to a halt.

"Get them, Gordon."

Jim quickly moved in front of Andi, shielding her with his body as Gordon reached inside his jacket and withdrew a handgun. A shot rang out, then another. Gordon dropped the gun. A cry of pain escaped his throat as he stumbled backward. Jim's head snapped around, his gaze frantically darting everywhere as he tried to figure out where the shots had come from and who had fired them. Then the world exploded around him.

Tires screeched on the pavement as two police cars skidded to a stop, their headlights illuminating the scene. He heard Steve yelling at someone to call the paramedics. A jerky movement off to the side grabbed his attention.

Buchanan knelt down and grabbed the weapon from where Gordon had dropped it on the pavement. Jim lunged toward him, knocking the gun from Milo's hand just as it discharged. He swung a clenched fist and connected squarely with Buchanan's jaw. Milo Buchanan sprawled backward across the sidewalk and stayed there.

Jim took a deep breath and then a second one as he tried to shove down the adrenaline surge and quiet the pounding in his chest. He became aware of the sharp twinges of pain in his left arm. He reached for it and felt the dampness. He withdrew his hand and stared in disbelief at the fresh smear of blood, only then realizing that Buchanan's wild shot had grazed his arm.

He spied the gun on the ground where it had fallen from Milo Buchanan's hand. He glanced off to one side where two policemen struggled with Gordon, who appeared to be putting up a good fight in spite of his wound. A third policeman helped a frail-looking Milo Buchanan to his feet. There did not seem to be anyone paying any attention to him. He reached down and grabbed the handgun.

As Jim turned back toward Andi, something in the shadows down the walkway caught his eye—a movement in an area that the angle of the car headlights could not illuminate. Then Andi's words of warning came rushing back at him, the words she had shouted just before the sound of the gun filled the air and she had fallen into his arms. Someone was still hidden from view...someone with a gun.

He glanced back at Andi. Some of the color had

come back into her face and she seemed to be breathing okay. She was out of sight from whoever continued to lurk in the shadows. He stepped away from the glare of the car lights and took a steadying breath. He extended a confident smile toward Andi.

She was injured but would be okay. The police were on the scene and the paramedics had been called. Milo Buchanan and Gordon were in police custody. That left only the other man on Milo's payroll—the person Benny had alluded to at their last meeting. Could that be the person hiding down the darkened walkway?

Jim stared at the gun in his hand. He had never shot at anyone in his life. He did not even like guns, but he did know how to use one.

He took one last look at the activity taking place on the street. Steve and another man flanked Benny. Steve had the briefcase back in his possession and another man stood with them—an older man whose face he could not see. It looked as if the confusion of a few minutes ago had been brought under control. That left only one last detail, the person who had shot Andi while trying to shoot him—the person hiding in the shadows down the walkway.

This was personal. Jim glanced at the policemen, all of whom seemed to be busy. Someone had given information to Milo Buchanan five years ago with the intention that Jim would be killed. That same person was still in the picture and presumably had just wounded Andi while making yet another attempt on his life. Yes, indeed—this whole thing was *very* personal.

He knelt down next to Andi and gently took her in his arms. He saw the pain on her face when she winced in reaction to his moving her. He forced a calm to his voice so as not to unnecessarily alarm her. "I'm sorry. I didn't mean to hurt you. Will you be okay here for a couple of minutes? I have something to take care of, then I'll be right back."

She attempted a smile, but did not quite make it. "It's all right. It doesn't hurt too bad." A frown wrinkled her brow and a hint of alarm entered her voice. "Your arm—"

He glanced at the rip in his shirt and the blood-stained fabric. "It's nothing, just a scratch. A bandage and I'll be good as new." He offered her a confident smile, brushed a loving kiss against her lips, then rose to his feet.

He checked the gun to make sure there were bullets in the clip and one in the chamber, then confirmed that the safety was off. A strange sense of calm settled over him, tempered with a warmth that came from a place of love. Andi had risked her life to save him. Whatever her involvement, whatever the past, none of it mattered. The only thing that counted was the here and now. And after five long years of not knowing what tomorrow would bring…at long last he could think about a future, and he knew that future included Andi.

But first he needed to take care of just one more thing. He turned toward the entrance to the walkway, flattened himself against the wall, then cautiously peered around the corner. He started to slip around the corner into the dark but paused as a thought struck him.

He turned back to Andi. "You know this area. The walkways between these buildings…is there another way to get to this one? Maybe around the outside of this building to the back?"

She shifted her weight slightly, a little gasp escaping her throat when she twisted her shoulder. "I'm not sure, why?'' Her gaze became riveted to the gun in his hand. ''Jim...'' She looked up at him, her face filled with her very real concern. ''What do you plan to do?''

Then the light of recognition came into her eyes and an urgency surrounded her words. ''No—you can't go down there.'' She glanced past him toward the police cars. ''Let the police do it. It's their job.''

Somewhere in the background he heard the sound of a siren. He returned his attention to the pleading in her eyes. ''Hang in there. I hear the paramedics.'' He smoothed her hair away from her face, then placed a tender kiss on her forehead. He looked into her eyes, the love he felt for her swelling in his heart. ''Andi...''

The barrel of the gun pressed against the back of Jim's head, sending a cold chill through his body. The words were filled with a combination of hate and desperation. ''You were a major obstacle to me back then, and now, five years later, you've pretty much signed an end to me and my plans. I don't have anything more to lose.''

Jim recognized the voice but could not place it. He swallowed his fear along with the lump in his throat. He slowly rose to his feet, not wanting to make any sudden moves. His primary concern at that moment was to move the danger away from Andi and stall for enough time to attract the attention of one of the policemen on the scene, all of whom seemed to be ignoring him while handling more pressing matters. He cautiously took a couple of steps sideways, then turned around to face his adversary.

''Frank Norton.'' Jim uttered the words in a very matter-of-fact tone of voice, showing neither surprise nor emotion. ''I should have known. You were the one I reported the bribe to and I never heard anything more about it. I guess that report went directly to Milo Buchanan rather than through proper channels.''

"Hands in the air, nice and easy."

The words came from directly behind Frank Norton. He stiffened to attention then hesitated. Jim saw the look dart across his face and settle in his eyes—the look that said a desperate man was about to do something very stupid.

"Now." The policeman's voice carried total authority and control. Frank blinked a couple of times, then let out a sigh of resignation. He handed the gun back over his shoulder. The policeman took it from him.

"Hands on your head." The policeman handed the gun to a fellow officer, then handcuffed Frank.

Jim breathed a sigh of relief as his gaze swept across the scene. He spotted the paramedics. He held his hand in the air and motioned to them. "Over here." He turned around to Andi. "You'll be fine now. These guys will take good care of you."

The paramedic placed his hand on Jim's arm. "Stand aside, please." He took a closer look at the rip in Jim's sleeve and the bloodstain. "Is this your only injury?"

"This is nothing, the bullet just grazed my arm. It's not much more than a scratch. Andi is the one who needs your attention."

"I'll get to you as soon as I finish here." He set his medical kit on the ground and knelt next to Andi.

JIM PLUMPED SOME EXTRA pillows against the headboard on Andi's bed, then helped her across the room. "There, now you can sit up and be comfortable." He pulled back the edge of the covers so she could slide into bed, then he sat down on the edge of the bed next to her. "Is there anything I can get for you? Anything you need?"

"What I *need* is for you to stop treating me like an invalid. The doctor said it was only a flesh wound. There's no infection, no nerve damage, nothing serious. They kept me in the hospital overnight for observation and sent me home this morning. In a few days I won't even know it happened."

He cupped her face in his hands and looked lovingly into her eyes. His voice filled with the emotion that had been bottled up inside him from the previous night, from the moment she had fallen into his arms when the bullet had struck her. "But *I'll* know it happened. Because of me you could have been killed. I'll never be able to erase the memory of the fear and panic that—"

"It most certainly was *not* your fault. If my memory is correct, clear back on Vancouver Island you're the one who told me to get on a plane and go home, to not get involved with you. I was the one who insisted that we do this. I was the one who pushed myself into the middle of everything over your very specific and emphatic objections."

He flashed a teasing grin as he reached out and tucked a loose strand of hair behind her ear. "So tell me…are you sorry that you were so pushy?" Before she could answer, he leaned his face into hers and captured her mouth with a loving kiss.

The sound of the doorbell interrupted the quiet moment of tenderness. Jim pulled back a little and gazed into her eyes. "Do you suppose if we ignore it, whoever it is will go away?"

As if in answer to his question, the doorbell sounded again. Jim let out a sign of resignation and rose from the edge of the bed. ''I'll get rid of whoever it is. You rest.''

Jim walked quickly through Andi's house and opened the front door. Steve Westerfall stood on the front porch with another man, someone else from Jim's past. He recognized him as Phil Herman.

Jim did not move aside, blocking the doorway so that the men could not come into the house. He glanced at Phil, then settled his gaze on Steve. ''Yes?''

A flash of irritation appeared on Steve's face. ''We'd like to come in. I need to talk to Andi, and I'm sure you probably have some questions for me.''

Jim stood his ground. ''Andi just got home from the hospital an hour ago. She's resting right now. Perhaps some other time.'' There was no mistaking the animosity in his voice.

''It's okay, Jim.'' Andi stepped into the living room from the hallway. ''I think I'd like to hear what Steve has to say.'' Andi's voice did not contain the same rancor as Jim's, but there was a noticeable combination of hurt and resentment that had never been there before when talking to Steve.

Jim moved aside so Steve and Phil Herman could come inside. The two men sat on the couch, Andi settled in the large easy chair and Jim rested on the chair arm next to her.

There was a moment of awkward silence as Jim and Andi stared at Steve, waiting for him to say something.

''I suppose I owe you—'' he made a gesture indicating both Jim and Andi ''—an explanation on what happened and why it went down the way it did.''

Andi leveled a steady look at him. ''Yes, I'd say you do.''

''Before I get to that, let me introduce you to Phil

Herman. Jim already knows him. Phil was the U.S. Attorney on the Buchanan case when it first came about. We've kept in touch over the years. Phil long suspected a leak inside his department and Frank Norton was his prime suspect, but there was no proof.''

Andi nodded her acknowledgment of Phil's presence, then waited for Steve to continue.

Phil provided some additional information. "When Jim disappeared out from under us and blew the case against Buchanan, I came under direct fire from those higher up, which I strongly suspected was fueled by someone on my staff. I had no choice but to accept personal blame and resign. I had no idea what happened, but I knew if at all possible I would one day see Milo Buchanan in jail. I really didn't know who I could trust in my office, or anywhere else for that matter, so I turned to Steve. I'd known him for several years and knew he was as passionate about seeing Milo behind bars as I was.''

Jim addressed his comment directly to Phil. "I assume Steve filled you in on what happened and why I took off. I'm sorry it cost you your job, but I had no other option.''

"Yes, Steve explained it to me. Had I been in your place, I would probably have done the same thing.''

"None of this explains why you lied to me, Steve.'' Andi's voice conveyed all the hurt that had lived inside her for the past few days. "You played me along just like one of your informants or contacts. And Jim...you used him knowing full well that his very life was in danger. I thought a ten-year relationship would mean more to you than that, but apparently I was wrong.''

Jim felt Andi's body begin to tremble from the emotional turmoil. He took her hand and gave it a little squeeze of reassurance.

"Andi…" Steve's gaze darted from her to Jim and then back to Andi again. "I heard it every time I talked to you while you were on the road. Then as soon as I saw the two of you together at the pub, I knew what the two of you probably didn't even know yet. And being around you for a couple of days only reinforced my opinion."

"What are you talking—" Andi paused when she heard Jim start talking at the same time.

"What does that—" Jim stopped in midsentence.

Steve seemed a little surprised by their reaction. "It was totally obvious that if the two of you weren't in love, you were at least well on your way. I knew there was no way in hell I could depend on either one of you to put your emotions aside and function logically. I could not afford the uncertainty of having to deal with either of you feeling you needed to protect the other."

Andi looked up at Jim at the same moment that he looked at her. Their gazes locked in a very intense moment of emotion. Each seemed to be silently asking the other the same question—was what Steve had just said the truth?

Steve managed to get in one more comment before completely losing their attention. "And even with all my planning, Andi still ended up with a bullet in her shoulder because she was somewhere she wasn't sup-posed to be."

Steve Westerfall and Phil Herman looked at each other, then they turned toward Jim and Andi, who were lost in their own world. Jim cradled Andi's head against his chest as he stroked her hair. There did not seem to be anything else for Steve to say, at least nothing that involved Jim and Andi. Phil and Steve left the house, pausing on the front porch for a few minutes of additional conversation.

"What about the money transfers?" Phil asked. "Without any proof I wasn't able to do anything about Buchanan's Cayman Islands accounts. I was somewhat limited in having access only to sources that would not get back to Frank."

Steve considered what Phil had said, then let out a soft chuckle. "I didn't think you'd be able to work around the system and the chain of command on that one, at least not in the tight time frame we had."

Phil looked at him curiously. "May I assume that evil little laugh of yours means that you've already done something about it?"

"It took a while, but my computer wiz finally cracked the numbered codes on Milo's accounts. She electronically transferred all the money out of his accounts—almost twelve million dollars—as soon as his flight took off. There was about a ten-minute time frame when he was totally isolated from any telephone or computer communication."

"Your computer wiz sounds like a real prize. Where did you find him?"

"*Her* name is Elena and she's a marvel—one really smart lady. If she weren't already happily married, and to my wife's brother..." Steve shot Phil a sly grin. "Well, no use speculating along those forbidden lines."

"Nice work. I'll let the Treasury Department figure what to do with the funds. The important thing is that the money is out of his reach. I imagine the IRS will put a freeze on the money as undeclared income for which he owes taxes. That should hold it for a while until we get this whole mess untangled." Phil glanced at his watch. "We'd better get going. There's lots of clean-up work to do. I can talk to Jim in a couple of days."

Steve glanced back over his shoulder at Jim and Andi. He fought the warm smile that tugged at the corners of his mouth. They were well suited for each other.

Andi watched as Steve and Phil stepped off the porch and crossed the lawn to Steve's car. She laced her fingers together with Jim's. "Well, it's all over. There's the trial, of course, but the danger is now in the past. The attempted murder and conspiracy to commit murder charges are here in California where Buchanan's influence is minimal at best." She felt a little shiver of trepidation. "What do you plan to do now? Have you thought about any plans?"

He considered her question. "Plans? This is a new concept for me. I don't know...I guess I'm sort of at a loss." He gazed lovingly into her eyes for a moment, then lowered his head and captured her mouth with a tender kiss. It only lasted for a few seconds, but it spoke volumes. "I thought I might delve a little deeper into what Steve had said—"

"About what Steve said..." Andi's voice trailed off as the emotion of the moment overwhelmed her.

"Andi...I can only speak for myself...." He nervously cleared his throat. "What he said is true. I love you, Andi. I'm not sure exactly where or when it happened, but it did."

She felt the warmth of his touch as the elation welled inside her. It was what she wanted to hear more than anything else. "It happened for me, too. I love you, Jim. I truly do."

The joy he felt at that moment surpassed anything he thought he would ever experience again. ''I never thought I'd ever again have someone to share my love with, someone who would love me in return. I'd just about given up hope of ever being able to lead a normal life again. I don't have a job or a home. I have nothing to offer you other than that love, but I give it to you freely, completely and forever.''

''You do have a home.'' Andi closed her eyes as a contented smile turned the corners of her mouth. ''It's right here with me.''